SEED-TIME AND HARVEST
and oth

THE ANNIVERSARY EDITION OF HERMAN CHARLES BOSMAN

Planning began in late 1997 – the fiftieth anniversary of Bosman's first collection in book form, Mafeking Road *– to re-edit his works in their original, unabridged and uncensored texts. The project should be completed by 2005 – the centenary of his birth.*

GENERAL EDITORS:
STEPHEN GRAY AND CRAIG MACKENZIE

Already published in this edition:
MAFEKING ROAD AND OTHER STORIES
WILLEMSDORP
COLD STONE JUG
IDLE TALK: VOORKAMER STORIES (I)
JACARANDA IN THE NIGHT
OLD TRANSVAAL STORIES
VERBORGE SKATTE

Herman Charles Bosman

SEED-TIME AND HARVEST
and other stories

The Anniversary Edition

Edited by Craig MacKenzie

HUMAN & ROUSSEAU
Cape Town Pretoria Johannesburg

Copyright © 2001 by The estate of Herman Charles Bosman
First published in 2001 by Human & Rousseau
28 Wale Street, Cape Town

Back cover photograph of Herman Charles Bosman in Johannesburg,
by an unknown street photographer, courtesy of the Harry Ransom Humanities Research Center
Photograph on front cover by David Goldblatt: *Harvest-time on the Koksoord Plots, Randfontein* (November 1962).
Design and typeset in 11 on 13 pt Times by ALINEA STUDIO, Cape Town
Printed and bound by NBD
Drukkery Street, Goodwood, Western Cape

ISBN 0 7981 4186 7

No part of this book may be reproduced or transmitted in any form or by any means,
electronic or mechanical or by photocopying, recording or microfilming, or stored in any
retrieval system, without the written permission of the publisher

Herman Charles Bosman was born near Cape Town in 1905, but moved with his family at an early age to the Transvaal, where he lived for most of his life. After training as a teacher he was posted in January, 1926, to a farm school near Zwingli in the Marico District of what was then the Western Transvaal. His stay there was abruptly terminated after he was arrested and convicted for the murder of his stepbrother during a vacation at the family home in Johannesburg. Initially condemned to hang, his sentence was commuted and he served four years in Pretoria Central Prison.

Upon his release he embarked on a career as a journalist and began writing short stories. Among his earliest works were Oom Schalk Lourens tales, which he wrote steadily between 1930 and 1951, the year of his death. Twenty of the total of sixty-one Oom Schalk stories appeared in *Mafeking Road* (1947), which Bosman himself saw into print. A further twenty appear here, in the order in which they were first published, with the remaining twenty-one scheduled for a third volume.

The first four stories in *Seed-time and Harvest* originally appeared in *The New LSD* and other satirical journals in 1931. The next five, written while the author was living in London (1934–1940), appeared mainly in the weekly *South African Opinion*. After a hiatus of four-and-a-half years, Bosman entered his most productive period, publishing the rest between 1944 and 1948 in the new monthly *S. A. Opinion* and in *Trek* and *On Parade*.

In this sequence one can see that he rapidly develops Oom Schalk from a wooden and overdetermining character into a subtle and well-organised narrator who always keeps the reader in suspense. Although a substantial amount of *Seed-time and Harvest* is early work, the volume contains rewarding items like "Marico Moon", "Dopper and Papist" and "Cometh Comet" – as well, of course, as the masterly title story itself.

Contents

Introduction 9

Veld Fire 21
Francina Malherbe 26
The Ramoutsa Road 31
Karel Flysman 37
Visitors to Platrand 42
Marico Moon 47
Bushveld Romance 52
On to Freedom 57
Martha and the Snake 62
Concertinas and Confetti 66
The Story of Hester van Wyk 73
The Wind in the Tree 80
Camp-fires at Nagmaal 86
Seed-time and Harvest 91
The Ghost at the Drift 97
Dopper and Papist 105
Cometh Comet 111
Graven Image 117
Great-uncle Joris 122
The Old Potchefstroom Gaol 127

Notes on the Text 133

Introduction

THROUGHOUT his career as a writer Herman Charles Bosman wrote short stories using his famous character, Oom Schalk Lourens, as his mouthpiece. There are sixty-one in all, produced between 1930 and 1951. When in 1946 he was suddenly presented with the chance of drawing together a one-volume selection from those he had written up to that date, he rather hastily assembled *Mafeking Road* (1947). This contained twenty Oom Schalks (with one story, "Brown Mamba", although also set in the Bushveld, using an authorial narrator). The volume was re-edited for the Anniversary Edition and appeared in 1998 as *Mafeking Road and Other Stories*, with the author's own selection and arrangement of the stories intact.

Thereafter two-thirds of the Oom Schalk stories were left uncollected, sufficient for another two volumes. At the time of his death Bosman was apparently in the process of gathering together another collection, with the intended title *Seed-time and Harvest*, after the key story here.

Then in 1963 when, thanks to the enduring success of *Mafeking Road*, Lionel Abrahams was encouraged to make one further selection, he had to limit the number of pieces he chose (finally Oom Schalks, with some other fine items), and his magnificent *Unto Dust* became popularly established in turn. Various other selections have since filled in some of the gaps.

For the Anniversary Edition, thanks to the success principally of *Mafeking Road* and *Unto Dust*, I have been given the opportunity that neither Bosman himself, nor Abrahams in his turn, were afforded: to gather together *all* of Bosman's short stories with the prospect of issuing them in a far less restricted and ad hoc way, and in volumes which naturally fall into categories, both generically and period-wise. For Oom Schalk we now have all of three volumes in which to contain the complete series, with two volumes for the complete Voorkamer series (only half of which have appeared before), and a further one for that third category of stories written with the authorial narrator (already published as *Old Transvaal Stories*).

So *Seed-time and Harvest* is the second of the projected three-part Oom Schalk series. The forty-one Oom Schalk stories remaining after Bosman made his selections for *Mafeking Road* have been arranged in order of date of publication and then divided into two roughly equal groups. *Seed-time and Harvest* contains the first twenty of these, printed in the order in which they first appeared. They span a considerable period of time: from "Veld Fire", first published in 1931 (and thus a very early Oom Schalk story) to "Great-uncle Joris", which first appeared in 1948. "Veld Fire" was written shortly after Bosman's release from prison, while "Great-uncle Joris" appeared after the publication of *Mafeking Road*, an event that marks Bosman's arrival as a published author of note.

The collection actually ends with "The Old Potchefstroom Gaol", a previously unpublished story found in near-finished, half-typescript half-holograph form in the archives of the Harry Ransom Humanities Research Center at the University of Texas at Austin. Like all of the other Bosman material there this manuscript was undated, so I felt at liberty – as it has an early feel about it – to publish it at the end of this sequence of Oom Schalk stories. (For a full account of the editing of this story see "Notes on the Text.")

The other previously unpublished story is "The Ghost at the Drift", also found in typescript form at the HRHRC, but as an Afrikaans version of the story appeared in *Die Brandwag* in April, 1948, it is readily dated. (No trace of an English publication has yet been found.) Two further stories, "Veld Fire" and "Martha and the Snake", have never before been collected in book form.

The remaining sixteen stories were originally published in *The Sjambok*, *The S. A. Opinion*, *Trek* and other periodicals in the 1930s and 1940s and were first collected variously in *Unto Dust* and in *Almost Forgotten Stories*. They are gathered together here in their original publication sequence for the first time.

One of the points of interest in the present volume is the development of Oom Schalk Lourens from an unnamed and undefined character to a larger-than-life presence in the later stories. Conspicuous in "Veld Fire", for example, is the absence of a distinctive narrative voice. The story appeared in *The Sjambok* (in 1939, its second printing) under the rubric "Life as Revealed by Fiction. . . " and was prefaced by an editorial note which presents it as an item of 'local colour': "A masterly short story of life on the veld, where victories of peace, more glorious than those of war, are often gained over drought and disease, over pests and privation." The story makes sparse use of direct speech and, but for a few pieces of distinctive Oom Schalk humour ("I thought. . . how fine it was to be born a woman, when you had nothing to do except stand in

Wilfrid Cross's illustration for "The Story of Hester van Wyk"
(The S. A. Opinion, June, 1944)

front of a fire and wash dishes, and tell your husband you're sorry you married him"), it is a fairly conventional first-person narrative.

Later stories deploy a more fully-fledged narrative agency: Oom Schalk becomes far more tangible as a presence and there are also clear textual signals that he is ostensibly engaging in an oral give-and-take with a circle of listeners and interlocutors. When one compares "Veld Fire" with, for example, "Bushveld Romance", one can see how Bosman developed a 'pitch-perfect' style of oral narration. With a minimum of authorial intervention the scene is set, and we conjure up a vivid image of a dissembling old raconteur, pipe in hand, holding forth to an implied audience.

The point is that Bosman consciously employed techniques to create the illusion of an oral style of delivery in his stories. The simplicity and idiomatic richness of his style, the easy pace at which the stories proceed, the use of leisurely digressions typical of oral tales told to an audience in which time is not of the essence. . . these are all devices used to foster the illusion that the medium of real, spoken language is being used. The stories therefore have the outward appearance of simplicity and artlessness and, indeed, as we shall shortly see, have been interpreted in this way, but there is a thoroughly modern economy and artfulness that permeates every aspect of Bosman's craft.

One example of a misinterpretation of Bosman's stories is an anonymous review of *Unto Dust* that appeared in *The Times Literary Supplement* (15 March, 1963):

> *Unto Dust* is a further collection of tales by the popular Afrikaner storyteller, Herman Charles Bosman. Bosman died in 1951 at the age of 46. He was once sentenced to death for murder, spent nine years in Europe in the 1930s, and worked as a journalist in South Africa. It is odd and anachronistic in the circumstances that he should have been able to make a reputation for himself by telling old tales of the Boer war, and that, considering his undoubted gifts, he should have wished to.
>
> The tales themselves seem authentic, old men's yarns that are likely enough to be told in an isolated, pioneering, bookless community: they serve an obvious purpose of whiling away the time. Yet in fact their appeal is to the deluded nostalgia of a very different community, and their seeming authenticity dissolves into pastiche. Bosman was an uncompromisingly backward writer, a poor Boer's, mid-twentieth-century Kipling.

Oddly enough, this inaccurate and patronising review is partly echoed by another appraisal closer to home. In a contemporaneous review of the short stories of Nadine Gordimer, Doris Lessing and Bosman, who were emerging as representatives of the post-war South African literary boom in the late 1940s, Joseph Sachs, having favourably reviewed the work of Gordimer and Lessing, turns to Bosman's *Mafeking Road* with the following words: "His simple unvarnished tales are more truly South African, than the intense and sophisticated writings of our other young writers" (*Trek*, November, 1951). He goes on to applaud Bosman for his "almost impersonal style" and his lack of "ideological luggage", and remarks that there "is all of South Africa in that little book."

Sachs's appreciation of Bosman's stories is sincere, and much of what he says in his review is well judged and accurate, but his tell-tale opening description of "simple unvarnished tales" in relation to the "intense and sophisticated" work of Gordimer and Lessing reveals his misapprehension of the sophistication and complexity of Bosman's art. Sachs's judgement in fact applies far better to the work of earlier South African pioneers of the oral-style form (W. C. Scully, J. Percy Fitz-Patrick and Ernest Glanville among them).

René Shapshak's illustration for "Concertinas and Confetti"
*(*The S. A. Opinion, *April, 1944)*

What is not immediately apparent is that Bosman used elements belonging to the two distinct genres of the fireside tale and the modern short story in fashioning his Bushveld stories. Fixing on the outward appearance of the stories, these critics fail to discern the new purposes to which an old genre is put. The words "authenticity", "old men's yarns", "deluded nostalgia" and "backwardness" (the *TLS* reviewer), and "simple unvarnished tales" (Sachs) reveal that both critics failed to see that Bosman infused an older art form with a modern sensibility. He took over the older genre of the fireside tale – for its qualities of intimacy and familiarity and its congruency with the milieu he wished to describe – but introduced into this familiar genre the new requirements of economy and trenchant social commentary.

These qualities are certainly in evidence in the stories gathered here. For example, Bosman seldom lets slip an opportunity to expose the venality of both predikant and politician, whose professions he clearly sees as being uncomfortably close to each other in nature. In "Marico Moon", the ouderling Petrus Lemmer quickly loses his façade of respectability when the mampoer takes effect, although to the end he maintains that "if he hadn't been at the dance he would like to know what would have happened." Hendrik Uys in "Concertinas and Confetti" secures his appointment as diaken by bribing the predikant with a pair of trek-oxen, and we

Abe Berry's illustration for "Seed-time and Harvest"
*(*On Parade, *1 Oct., 1948)*

then hear that "the part he was playing in politics was already of such a character as to make more than one person regard him as a prospective candidate for the Volksraad." And the ouderling in "Seed-time and Harvest" begins visiting the wife of a man who has been forced to leave his farm with his cattle because of drought, and is then reported to remark piously that "it must be the Lord's will that this drought had descended on the Marico, and that. . . in spite of what people might think he would be as pleased as anybody else when the rains came again."

But Bosman reserves his strongest satire of the church for "Dopper and Papist", which recounts a journey Schalk Lourens undertakes to Zeerust in the presence of a predikant and an ouderling. At one point he overhears the two men "discussing theology": "'You never saw such a lot of brandsiek sheep in your life,' the predikant was saying, 'as what Chris Haasbroek brought along as tithe.'" After overhearing another such item on "an abstruse point of religion" – this time revealing the predikant's intention to blackmail the chairman of the Meat Board to ensure that his son is appointed an anthrax inspector – Schalk remarks

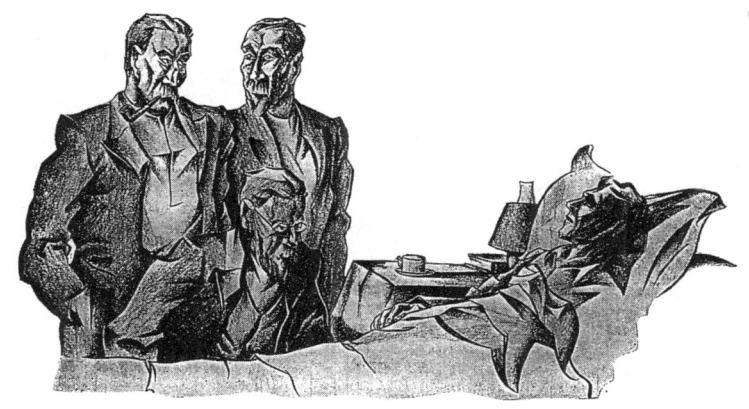

Wilfrid Cross's illustration for "Visitors to Platrand"
(The S. A. Opinion, *1 Nov., 1935)*

poker-faced: "I realised then that you could find much useful guidance for your everyday problems in the conversation of holy men."

Bosman is similarly acerbic in his treatment of the supposed military prowess of the Boers. In "Karel Flysman", the story about a cowardly man who crawls away on hands and knees as soon as an engagement starts, he satirises the much-vaunted 'guerilla tactics' that the Boers adopted in the Anglo–Boer War. And the callowness and parochialism of the commandos, their lack of discipline and their disorganisation, is mercilessly lampooned in "Great-uncle Joris", in which a vainglorious commando is ignominiously put to flight ("To reload, we said, years afterwards, to strangers who asked") by a few unexpected volleys of rifle fire from a black tribe.

This clearly satirical dimension notwithstanding, the stories are also frequently elliptical. It is as if Bosman, having adroitly exposed the oddities of human behaviour, is content to step back and tacitly declare human nature ultimately to be a mystery. What causes Francina Malherbe to break so dramatically from her conventional, church-going routine? Why does the backveld throw up such anomalies as Paulus Oberholzer ("The Ramoutsa Road"), who writes poetry, turns his back on his community and 'goes native'? What actually happens to Frik Engelbrecht ("Visitors to Platrand") when he and his prospective brother-in-law, Koenrad Wium, go deep into the Bechuanaland Protectorate? And how much does Lettie Wium know about the fate of her lover?

What causes young Annie ("Marico Moon") to burst into tears at the

Maurice van Essche's illustration for "Camp-fires at Nagmaal"
(The S. A. Opinion, *June, 1945)*

end of the story? Why should Minnie Bonthuys fall in love with a man who seems so utterly unsuited to her ("Bushveld Romance")? What precisely is "that stillness of the body and the spirit" possessed by both Marie Snyman and her daughter Annette? And who is the young man jilted at the end by Annette ("Concertinas and Confetti")? Why does Schalk Lourens remark that Hester van Wyk was "a very pretty girl", but that when "you were close enough to her to see what was in her eyes" you realised that "no child had ever smiled like that"? Why does Petrus Steyn choose to trek right through the Kalahari and on to Angola ("Camp-fires at Nagmaal") when he is in love with a girl who waits for him in the Marico?

But perhaps the most tantalising lacuna of all is the explanation for the cuckold Jurie Steyn's warm relationship with his (almost certainly) bastard son ("Seed-time and Harvest"). It is the unexpected and the unpredictable that appeal so much to Bosman. The moment of transcendence at the end of this story, when Jurie Steyn gently takes his son's hand, and Oom Schalk is moved to give up his petty squabble with Jurie over fence-poles and barbed wire, is vintage Bosman: "I somehow felt that there were more important things in life than the question of what had happened to my roll of barbed wire at Ramoutsa. And more important things than what had happened about the ouderling from near Vleisfontein."

Reg Turvey's illustration for "Seed-time and Harvest"
(The S. A. Opinion, *Dec., 1946*)

It is towards this elusive significance in human affairs – a significance that always remains just beyond the reach of language – that Bosman strives in this remarkable collection of stories. Like the seasonal cycles in the landscape on which they struggle to wrest a living, his characters seem destined to live out their lives according to some

Donald Harris's illustration for "The Wind in the Tree"
(The S. A. Opinion, *Jan., 1945*)

Illustration accompanying "Cometh Comet"
*(*Trek*, June 1948; artist unknown)*

inexorable pattern. Annie will probably follow the sad pattern of unrequited love set by her stepmother's brother, Petrus Lemmer ("Marico Moon"). Annette is fated to inherit her mother's enigmatic disposition – a disposition that will ensure that she remains forever beyond her husband's conceptual grasp ("Concertinas and Confetti"). Gerrit van Biljon needs to replicate a romantic context by planting bluegums, the species of tree under which he first won his wife's love ("The Wind in the Tree"), while Jan Bezuidenhout meets the same grisly end as his Great-uncle Joris, and leaves his widow to another man's attentions.

In "Cometh Comet", however, this patterning achieves an ancient resonance. Here the biblical nativity story is rendered in Bushveld burlesque. Bosman's point once again is that, while our material contexts may change through time, there is something constant (and endearing) in human foibles and follies. It is as if his characters are resigned to take their place in the ineluctable cycles promised by God to Noah after the flood: "While the earth remaineth, seed-time and harvest, and cold and heat, and summer and winter, and day and night shall not cease" (Genesis 8:22) – the passage referred to more than once in these stories.

Although we cannot be sure of Bosman's intention in planning a collection of his stories under this title, in giving it to this second volume of Oom Schalks after *Mafeking Road* we cannot be going too far adrift from what he desired.

Craig MacKenzie
Johannesburg, 2001

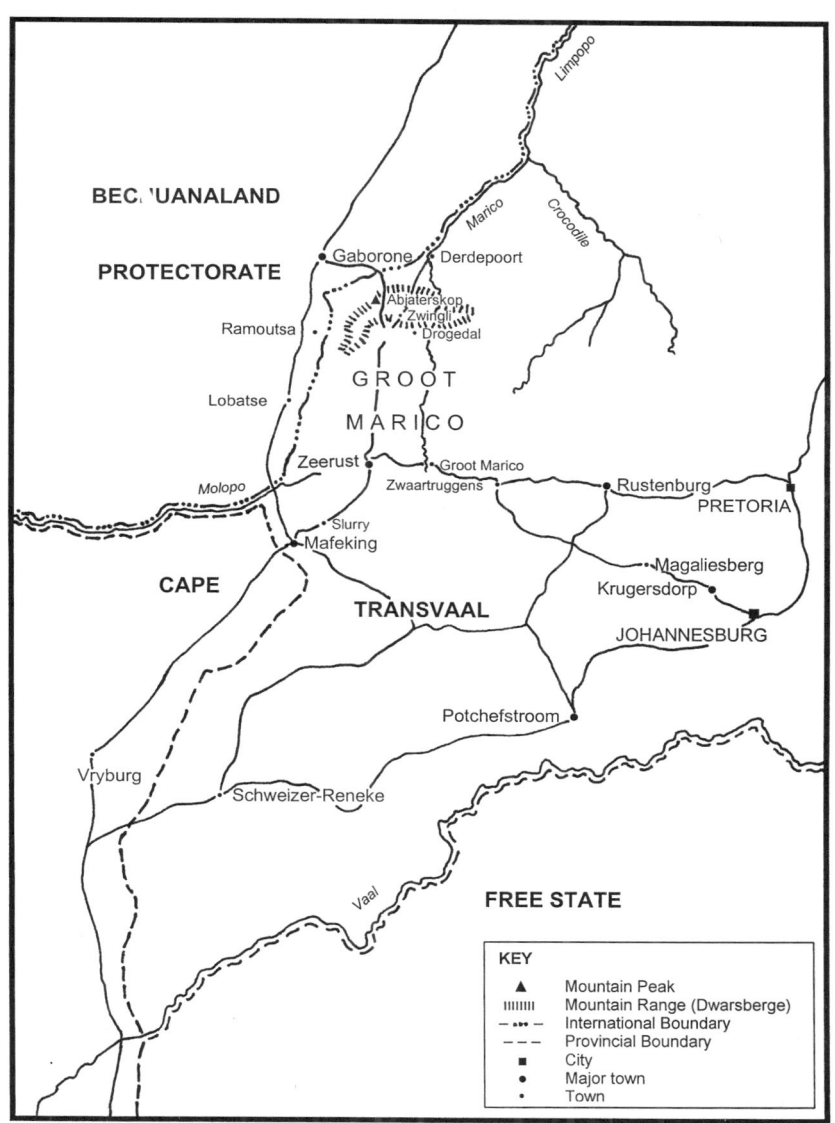

Oom Schalk Lourens's Western Transvaal

Veld Fire

I LET go the pump-handle and took off my hat.

It was very hot, and the sweat stood out on my forehead and ran down my cheeks. I looked across the laagte where my house stood in the cool of the kameeldorings. I wanted all sorts of things, then. I wanted rain so that the pans would be full, and there would be no more need for me to stand pumping water for the cattle all day long. I also wanted more cows and oxen, but then I remembered that if I had more cattle I would also have to pump more water for them. So I wasn't too sure. I even felt slightly pleased to think that in July the kaffirs had stolen six of my Afrikaner cows. It was funny to think of the way they would have to sweat, pumping water, for Afrikaner cows can drink a lot.

The house seemed very pleasant. A kaffir was chopping up a fallen trunk for firewood. That looked easier work to me than pumping water. Only the kaffir was not doing it properly. He had only a chopper with a short handle, and he stood over the wood with his body bent double. Of course, the right way to chop wood when the handle is short like that is to sit down on the grass beside the woodpile. When the handle is longer you can sit on a paraffin box. But only an ignorant Bechuana kaffir would stand. Also, when you are sitting on the ground you can nearly always rest your back against a big rock. That is why the Lord scattered so many ironstone boulders right through the Marico Bushveld. From what I know of farming today, I would never think of buying a farm without first making sure that it is full of large-sized stones.

I lit my pipe and then went on and started afresh with the pump-handle, but no matter how hard I tried, I couldn't think of an easy way of doing pumping.

"Kleinbooi," I shouted.

The kaffir put down the chopper and came across to the pump.

"You pump water, Kleinbooi," I said. "You're no use at chopping wood. And don't leave here until the drinking-place is full."

I walked through the long grass towards the woodpile. It was late in August and the grass was long and yellow and dry. In some spots it came almost up to my chest, and when I left the path to get to the wood I trampled a long swath of grass underfoot. It was eleven o'clock in the morning and in spite of the light wind blowing the heat was oppressive. I saw then that I couldn't possibly chop any of the wood before I had first gone into the house for a cup of coffee.

So I went round the house to the kitchen. I saw coffee which my wife had poured out for me, and while I smoked I thought of all that wood and of the pump-handle, with the knot in it near the end that blistered the inside of your hand, and of the way the sun burnt the back of your neck when you stooped down and of how fine it was to be born a woman, when you had nothing to do except stand in front of a fire and wash dishes, and tell your husband you're sorry you married him.

"It's a bad job, pumping water for all that cattle," I said to my wife. "It gives me a pain just here, in the small of my back."

I drank another cup of coffee, after which I took up my hat and walked slowly to the kitchen door.

"God," I said. "Oh, God". . . just like that. The kaffir Kleinbooi had left the pump. And the cattle had also gone.

For the whole of that part of the veld was one long sheet of flame. The sparks from the tobacco I had struck out of my pipe must have fallen on a blade of grass. Even as I stood and watched the fire spread rapidly further. I called the kaffirs but it was not necessary to call them. They had all seen the fire, and knowing it was useless to try and fight against it, had run away.

"We've got to save the house," I shouted.

One or two of the kaffirs came to help me, but the rest of them had hurried off to their own huts to stop the fire from burning down their thatched roofs. Right down to the foot of the koppies in front of my house the veld was in a blaze. Koen van Rensburg, my nearest neighbour, had seen the fire from the road along which he happened to be travelling to Ramoutsa. He left his donkey-cart on the road and came running down to help me. Between us we managed to get the kaffirs away from their own homes. Although they were my kaffirs, yet then they obeyed Koen more readily than they did me. For when he got off the wagon he brought the donkey-whip with him.

We hastened into the storeroom and emptied half a dozen sacks of mealies on to the floor. The most we could hope to do then was to save the house. Therefore I made the kaffirs take a sack each and light it at one end. I wanted to make a fireguard around the house by burning a wide stretch of grass over which the fire from the veld would not be able to leap. We burnt a few feet of grass at a time, and then beat it out again quickly, before it had time to spread, but the grass was so dry and long that several times our own fire nearly got out of hand. Still, we managed to make the fireguard. I worked alongside the kaffirs while Koen superintended with the donkey-whip. When we had finished this task, so that round the house there was a ten-yards breadth of blackened grass, we noticed that all the kaffir women with their children were gathered together at the back of my house. Their huts had gone up in flames and they themselves had just managed to get away in time, with the exception of a blind and crippled woman of about ninety, whom they were probably glad to leave behind.

Then, also, for the first time we saw Koen van Rensburg's donkey-cart had gone. Terrified by the smoke and flames the donkeys had stampeded with the cart. Fortunately, they had taken a safe direction. For now the fire could only spread one way, and that was towards the Bechuanaland Protectorate. On one side was the Dwarsberg mountains; on the other ran the Government Road, which all its length was very wide and grew wider every year, on account of the farmers always driving on the outside of it to avoid the potholes in the middle. Accordingly, the fire would not be able to cross the road.

With a fair wind behind them, the flames raced on through the bushes and long grass. They swept along between the road and the hills over a breadth of more than seven miles. Koen and I had caught a couple of horses which had been grazing on that part of the veld that lay below the pump, and we set off over the black and still smoking grass to follow the progress of the fire.

"Man, this is bad," Koen shouted, "all those farms in the Protectorate. Lucky!"

He stopped talking, but I knew he was going to say that he was glad his own farm lay behind us and could not be touched by the fire. And although he had helped me very much, yet I hated Koen for wanting to say that.

We rode fast, for horses are more tender in the hoof than donkeys, and, of their own accord, the two horses we were riding travelled as hard as they could go with the hot grass making things uncomfortable for them.

When we got near the fire we heard the roar of the flames eating up the grass and as they caught the trees they crackled the dry twigs and leaves and branches. In a single flash a long red flame would spring from the grass to the top of a tall tree. You could see the whole tree wilt in one moment with its head wrapped in a huge sheet of fire that roared and blazed with the wind behind it. In almost that same moment the tree would be burnt out, standing black and lifeless, its branches dropping straight downwards, like the coat-sleeves of an armless man.

Millions of sparks danced together in the wind. The smell of smoke made my nostrils smart. For seven miles that high wall of flame ran over the veld.

We came across numbers of dead springhares that had tried to break through the flames. I was glad that the cattle had more sense than to try to do that. The fire was travelling quickly, but as the wind had veered the cattle would be able to keep ahead quite easily, especially as they had a long start.

Koen and I rode slowly after the fire. Near us something jumped out through the flames and fell on an ant-hill, a kicking bundle of burnt flesh. It was a duiker lamb. By the time it struck the ant-hill it had already stopped moaning. Koen jumped off his horse and looked at the lamb, but by the time he got there the animal had not only left off moaning; it was no longer kicking either. It looked as though it had been roasted in an oven. Nothing could pass through that fire and live.

"Poor thing," Koen said. He always had a soft heart that way.

It is strange how, in big matters, you can only think of one thing at a time. It is always like that, whether anthrax breaks out on your farm, or the lightning kills your cattle, or the wild-dogs are in your sheep-kraal, or you suddenly find out that the new minister is an agent for a company in his spare time, and is trying to insure you.

So it was with the fire. Today I can hardly believe that then I was so short-sighted. All I was able to think of was saving the house. When I had done that I saw in which direction the wind was blowing, and I was satisfied that the cattle would be able to keep on ahead of the flames. Then suddenly I remembered.

"Koen," I said, "let us go home."

Koen looked at me in surprise.

"Why, what is the matter?" he asked.

"Nothing," I replied. "Only, after this I won't need to pump so much water."

Then we turned back home, riding very slowly.

You see, what I had forgotten, up to that moment, was that at the end of my farm there was a barbed-wire fence through which the cattle could not go. And as the fire was travelling then it would reach the fence in about half an hour.

Koen van Rensburg left me at my front door and went on alone to look after his donkey-cart.

That night my wife and I stood at the pump a long while and looked out towards the Bechuanaland Protectorate. It was a dark night. Far in the west there were faint crimson streaks against the skyline, where the fire was dying on the hills.

Francina Malherbe

After her father's death, Oom Schalk Lourens said, Francina Malherbe was left alone on the farm Maroelasdal. We all wondered then what she would do. She was close on to thirty, and in the Bushveld, when a girl is not married by twenty-five, you can be quite certain that she won't get a man anymore. Unless she has got money. And even then if she gets married at about thirty she is liable to be left afterwards with neither money nor husband. Look at what happened to Grieta Steyn.

But with Francina Malherbe it was different.

I remember Francina as a child. She was young when Flip first trekked into the Bushveld. There was an unlucky man for you. Just the year after he had settled on Maroelasdal the rinderpest broke out and killed off all his cattle. That was a bad time for all of us. But Flip Malherbe suffered most. Then, for the first time that anybody in the Marico District could remember, a pack of wolves came out of the Kalahari, driven into the Transvaal by the hunger. For in the Kalahari nearly all the game had died with the rinderpest. Maroelasdal was the nearest farm to the border, and in one night, as Flip told us, the wolves got into his kraal and tore the insides out of three hundred of his sheep. This was all the more remarkable, because Flip, to my knowledge, had never owned more than fifty sheep.

Then Flip Malherbe's wife died of the lung disease, and shortly afterwards also his two younger sons who were always delicate. That left only Francina, who was then about fifteen. All those troubles turned Flip's head a little. That year the Government voted money for the relief of farmers who had suffered from the rinderpest, and Flip put in a claim. He got paid quite a lot of money, but he spent most of it in Zeerust on drink. Then Flip went to the school-teacher and asked him if the Government would not give him compensation also because his wife and his sons had died, but the teacher, who did not know that Flip had become strange in the head, only laughed at him. Often after that, Flip told us that he was sorry his wife and children had died of the lung disease instead of the rinderpest, because otherwise he could have put in a claim for them.

Francina left school and set to work looking after the farm. With what was left out of the money Flip had got from the Government, she bought a few head of cattle. When the rains came she bought seed mealies and set the kaffir squatters ploughing in the vlakte. For three months in the year, by law, the kaffirs have to work for the white man on whose land they live. But you know what it is with kaffirs. As soon as they saw that there was no man on the farm who would see to it that they worked, the kaffirs ploughed only a little every day for Flip and spent the rest of the time in working for themselves. Francina spoke to her father about it, but it was no good. Flip just sat in front of the house all day smoking his pipe. In the end, Francina wrote out all the trek-passes and made all the kaffirs clear off the farm, except old Mosigo, who had always been a good kaffir.

In those days, Francina was very pretty. She had dark eyes with long lashes that curled down on her red cheeks when her eyes were closed. I know, because I usually sat near her in church, and during prayers I sometimes looked sideways at her. That was sinful, but then I was not the only one who did it. Whenever I opened my eyes slightly to look at her, I saw that there were other men doing the same thing. Once a young minister, who had just finished his studies at Potchefstroom, came to preach to us, so that we could appoint him as our predikant if we wished. But we did not appoint him. The ouderlings and diakens in the church council said that perhaps they could permit a minister to look underneath his lids while he was praying, but it was only right that his eyes should be shut all the time when he pronounced the blessing.

For the next two years I don't know how Francina and her father managed to make a living on the farm. But they did it somehow. Also, after a while they got other kaffir families to squat on the farm, and to help Mosigo on the lands with the ploughing time. Once Flip left his place on the front stoep and got into the mule-cart and drove to Zeerust. After two days, the hotel proprietor sent him back to the farm on an Indian trader's wagon. Flip had sold the mules and cart and bought drink.

Shortly after that I saw Flip at the post office. The dining room of Hans Welman's house was the post office, and we all went there to talk and fetch our letters. Flip came in and shook hands with everybody in the way we all did, and said good morning. Then he went up to Hans Welman and held out his hand. Welman just looked Flip Malherbe up and down and walked away. But with all his nonsense, Flip was sane enough to know that he had been insulted.

"You go to hell, Hans Welman," he shouted.

Welman turned round at once.

"My house is the public post office," he said, "so I can't throw you out. But I can say what I think of you. You treat your daughter like a kaffir. You're a low, drunken mongrel."

We could see that Flip Malherbe was afraid, but he could do nothing else after what the other man had said to him. So he went up to Welman and hit him on the chest. Welman just laughed and grabbed Flip quickly by the collar. Then he ran with him to the door, spun him round and kicked him under the jacket.

"Filth," he said, when Flip fell in the dust.

We all felt that Hans Welman had no business to do that. After all, it was Flip's own affair as to how he treated his daughter.

After that we rarely saw Flip again. He hardly ever moved from his front stoep. At first young men still came to call on Francina. But later on they stopped coming, for she gave them no encouragement. She said she could not marry while her father was still alive as she had to look after him. That was usually enough for most young men. They had only to glance once at Flip, who of late had grown fat and hearty-looking, to be satisfied that it would still be many years before they could hope to get Francina. Accordingly, the young men stayed away.

By and by nobody went to the Malherbes' house. It was no use calling on Flip, because we all knew he was mad. Although, often, when I thought of it, it seemed to me that he was less insane than what people believed. After all, it is not every man who can so arrange his affairs that he has nothing more to do except to sit down all day smoking and drinking coffee.

But although Francina never visited anybody, yet she always went regularly to church. Only, as the years passed, she became faded and no more young men looked at her during prayers. There were other and younger girls whom they would look at now. She had become thinner and there were wrinkles under her eyes. Also, her cheeks were no longer red. And there are always enough fresh-looking girls in the Bushveld, without the young men having to trouble themselves overmuch about those who have grown old.

And so the years passed, as you read in the Book, summer and winter and seed-time and harvest.

Then one day Flip Malherbe died. The only people at the funeral were the Bekkers, the Van Vuurens, my family and Hendrik Oberholzer, the ouderling who conducted the service. We saw Francina scatter dust over her father's face and then we left.

That was the time when we began to wonder what Francina would do. It was fifteen years since her mother had died, so that Francina was now thirty, and during those fifteen years she had worked hard and in a careful way, so that the farm Maroelasdal was all paid and there were plenty of sheep and cattle, and every year they sowed many sacks of mealies. But Francina just went on exactly the same as she had done when her father was still alive. Only, now the best years of a woman's life were behind her, and during all that time she had had nothing but work. We all felt sorry for her, the womenfolk as well, but there was nothing we could do.

Francina came to church every Sunday, and that was about the only time that we saw her. Yet both before and after church she was always alone, and she seldom spoke to anybody. In her black mourning dress she began to look almost pretty again, but of what use was that at her age?

People who had trekked into the Marico District in the last four years and only knew her by sight said she must also be a little strange in the head, like her father was. They said it looked as though it was in the family. But we who saw her grow up knew better. We understood that it was her life that had made her lonely like that. On account of having to look after her father she had missed much.

One day an insurance agent came through the Bushveld. He called at all the houses, Francina's also. It did not seem as if he was doing much business in the district, and yet every time he came back. And people noticed that it was always to Francina's house that the insurance agent went first. They talked about it. The old people shook their heads in the way that old people do when, although they don't know for sure about a thing, yet all the same they would like to believe it is so.

But if Francina knew what was being said about her she never mentioned it to anybody, and she didn't try to act differently. Nevertheless, there came a Sunday when she missed going to church. At once everybody felt that what was being whispered about her was true. Especially when she did not come to church the next Sunday or the Sunday after. Of course, stories that are told in this way about women are always true. But there was one thing that they said that was a lie. They said that what the insurance agent wanted was Francina's farm and cattle. And they foretold that exactly the same thing would happen to

Francina as had happened to Grieta Steyn: that in the end she would lose both her property and the man.

As I have told you, this last part of their stories did not come out in the way they had prophesied. If the insurance agent really had tried to get from her the farm and the cattle, nobody could say for sure. But what we did know was that he had gone back without them. He left quite suddenly, too, and he did not return anymore.

And Francina never again came to church. Yes, it's funny that women should get like that. For I did not imagine that anything could ever come across Francina's life that would make her go away from her religion. But, of course, you can't tell.

Sometimes when I ride past Maroelasdal in the evening, on my way home, I wonder about these things. When I pass that point near the aardvark mound, where the trees have been chopped down, and I see Francina in front of the house, I seem to remember her again as she was when she was fifteen. And if the sun is near to setting, and I see her playing with her child, I sometimes wish, somehow, that it was not a bastard.

The Ramoutsa Road

YOU'LL see that grave by the side of the road as you go to Ramoutsa, Oom Schalk Lourens said.

It is under that clump of withaaks just before you get to the Protectorate border. The kaffirs are afraid to pass that place at night.

I knew Hendrik Oberholzer well. He was a good man. Unlike most of the farmers who lived here in those days, Hendrik Oberholzer was never caught smuggling cattle across the line. Perhaps it was because he was religious and would not break the law. Or else he chose only dark nights for the work. I don't know. I was rather good at bringing cattle over myself, and yet I was twice fined for it at Zeerust.

Hendrik Oberholzer lived on the farm Paradyskloof. When he first trekked in here he was already married and his son Paulus was about fourteen. Paulus was a lively youngster and full of spirits when there was drought in the land and there was no ploughing to be done. But when it rained, and they had to sow mealies, Paulus would be sulky for days. Once I went to Paradyskloof to borrow a sack of cement from Hendrik for a sheep-dip I was building. Paulus was on the lands, walking behind the plough. I went up and spoke to him, and told him about the cement for the sheep-dip. But he didn't stop the oxen or even turn his head to look at me. "To hell with you and your cement," he shouted.

Then he added, when he got about fifteen yards away, "And the sheep-dip."

For some time after that Hendrik Oberholzer and I were not on speaking terms. Hendrik said that he was not going to allow other men to thrash his son. But I had only flicked Paulus's bare leg with the sjambok. And that was after he had kicked me on the shin with his veldskoen, because I had caught him by the wrist and told him that he wasn't to abuse a man old enough to be his father. Anyway, I didn't get the cement.

Then, a few days before the minister came up to hold the Nagmaal, Hendrik called at my house and said we must shake hands and forgive one another. As he was the ouderling, the predikant stayed with him for three days, and if he was at enmity with anybody, Hendrik would not be allowed to share in the Nagmaal. I was pleased to have the quarrel settled. Hendrik Oberholzer was an upright man whom we all respected for his Christian ways, and he also regularly passed on to me the Pretoria newspapers after he had finished reading them himself.

Afterwards, as time went by, I could see that Hendrik was much worried on account of his son. Paulus was the only son of Hendrik and Lettie. I know that often Hendrik had sorrowed because the Lord had given him no more than one child, and yet this one had strange ways. Because of that, both Hendrik and his wife Lettie became saddened.

Paulus had had a good education. His father didn't take him out of school until he was in Standard Four. And for another thing, he had been to Sunday school since he was seven. Also his uncle, who was a builder, had taught Paulus to lay flat stones for stoeps. So, taken all round, Paulus had more than enough learning for a farmer. But he was not content with that. He said he wanted to learn. Hendrik Oberholzer reasoned with him and, very fairly and justly, pointed out to him what had happened to Piet Slabberts. Piet Slabberts had gone to high school, and when he came back he didn't believe in God. So nobody was surprised when, two months later, Piet Slabberts fell off an ox-wagon and was killed by the wheels going over his head.

But Paulus only laughed.

"That is not so wonderful," he said. "If an ox-wagon goes over your head you always die, unless you've got a head like a Bushman's. If Piet Slabberts didn't die, only then would I say it was wonderful."

Yes, it was sinful of Paulus to talk like that when we could all see that in that happening was the hand of God. At the funeral the ouderling who conducted the service also spoke about it, and Piet Slabberts's mother cried very much to think that the Lord had taken away her son because He was not satisfied with him.

Anyway, Paulus did less work on the farm. Even when the dam dried up, and for weeks they had to pump water for the cattle all day out of the borehole, Paulus just looked on and only helped when his father and the kaffirs could not do any more. And yet he was twenty and a strong, well-built young man. But there was something in him that was bad.

At first Hendrik Oberholzer had tried to make excuses for his son, saying that he was young and had still to learn wisdom, but later on he spoke no more about Paulus. Hendrik's wife Lettie also said nothing. But there was always sadness in her eyes. For Paulus was her only child and he was not like other sons. He would often take a piece of paper and a pencil with him and go away in the bush and write verses all day. Of course Hendrik tore up those bits of paper whenever he found them in the house. But that made no difference. Paulus just went on with his sinful, worldly things, even after the minister had spoken to him about it and told him that no good could come out of writing verses – unless they were hymns. But even then it was foolish. Because in the hymn-book there were more hymns than people could use.

Instead of starting to work for himself and finding some girl to whom he could get married, Paulus, as I have said, just loafed about. Yet he was not bad-looking and there were many girls who could have favoured him if he looked at them first. And from them he could have chosen a woman for himself. Only Paulus took no notice of girls and seemed shy in their company.

One afternoon I went over to Hendrik Oberholzer's farm to fetch back a saw that I had bought from him. But Hendrik and Paulus had gone to Zeerust with a load of mealies, so that when I got to the house only Hendrik's wife Lettie was there. I sat down and talked to her for a little while. By and by, after she had poured out the coffee, she started talking about Paulus. She was very grieved about him and I could see that she was not far off crying. Therefore I went and sat next to her on the riempiesbank, and did my best to comfort her.

"Poor woman. Poor woman," I said and patted her hand. But I couldn't comfort her much, because all the time I had to keep an eye on the door in case Hendrik came in suddenly.

Then Lettie showed me a few bits of paper that she had found under Paulus's pillow. It was the same kind of verses that he had been writing for a long time, all about mimosa trees and clouds and veld flowers and that sort of nonsense. When I read those things I felt sorry that I didn't hit him harder with the sjambok that day he kicked me on the shin.

"He does not work even as much as a piccanin," Hendrik's wife Lettie said. "All day he writes on these bits of paper. I can't understand what is wrong with him."

"A man who writes things like that will come to no good," I said to her. "And I am sorry for you. It is not good the way Paulus is treating you."

Immediately Lettie turned on me like one of those yellow-haired wild-cats, and told me I had no right to talk about her son. She said I ought to be ashamed of myself and that, no matter what Paulus was like, he was always a much better man than any impudent Dopper who dared to talk about him. She said a lot of other things besides, and I was pleased when Hendrik returned. But I saw then how much Lettie loved Paulus. Also, it just shows you that you never know where you are with a woman.

Then one day Paulus went away. He just left home without saying a word to anybody.

Hendrik Oberholzer was very much troubled. He rode about to all the farms around here and asked if anyone had seen his son. He also went to Zeerust and told the police, but the police did not do much. All they ever did was to get our people fined for bringing scraggy kaffir cattle across the line. The sergeant at the station was a raw Hollander who listened to everything Hendrik said, and then at the end told Hendrik, after he had written something in a book, that perhaps what had happened was that Paulus had gone away.

Of course, Hendrik came to me, and I did what I could to help him. I went up to the Marico River right to where it flows into the Limpopo, and from there I came back along the Bechuanaland Protectorate border. Everywhere I enquired for Paulus. I was many days away from the farm.

I had hardly got back home when Hendrik called for news. From his lands he had seen me come through the poort and he had hastened over to see me.

We sat down in the voorkamer and filled our pipes.

"Well, Lourens," Hendrik said, and his eyes were on the floor, "have you heard anything about Paulus?"

It was early afternoon, with the sun shining in through the window, and in Hendrik's brown beard were white hairs that I had not noticed before.

I saw how Hendrik looked at the floor when he asked about his son. So I told him the truth, for I could see then that he already knew.

"The Lord will make all things right," I said.

"Yes, God knows what is best," Hendrik Oberholzer answered. "I heard about — They told me yesterday."

Hendrik could not bring himself to say that which we both knew about his son.

For, on my way back along the Bechuanaland border, I had come across Paulus. It was in some Mtosa huts outside Ramoutsa. There were about a dozen huts of red clay standing in a circle amongst the bushes. In front of each hut a kaffir lay stretched out in the sun with a blanket over him. All day long these kaffirs lie there in the sun, smoking dagga and drinking beer. Their wives and children sow the kaffir-corn and the mealies and look after the cattle. And with no clothes on, but just a blanket over him, Paulus also lay amongst those kaffirs. I looked at him only once and turned away, without knowing whether he had seen me.

Next to him a kaffir woman sat stringing white beads on to a piece of copper wire.

That was what I told Hendrik Oberholzer.

"It would be much better if he was dead," Hendrik said to me. "To think that a son of mine should turn kaffir."

That was very terrible. Hendrik Oberholzer was right when he said it would be better if Paulus was dead.

I had known before of low-class Uitlanders going to live in a kraal and marrying kaffir women and spending the rest of their lives sleeping in the sun and drinking bujali. But that was the first time I had heard of that being done by a decent Boer son.

Shortly afterwards Hendrik left. He said no more about Paulus, except to let me know that he no longer had a son. After that I didn't speak about Paulus either.

In a little while all the farmers in the Groot Marico knew what had happened, and they talked much of the shame that had come to Hendrik Oberholzer's family. But Hendrik went on just the same as always, except that he looked a great deal older.

Things continued in that way for about six months. Or perhaps it was a little longer. I am not sure of the date, although I know that it was shortly after the second time that I had to pay ten pounds for cattle-smuggling.

One morning I was in the lands talking to Hendrik about putting some more wires on the fence, so that we wouldn't need herds for our sheep, when a young kaffir on a donkey came up to us with a note. He said that Baas Paulus had given him that note the night before, and had told him to bring it over in the morning. He also told us that Baas Paulus was dead.

Hendrik read the note. Then he tore it up. I never got to learn what Paulus had written to him.

"Will you come with me, Lourens?" he asked.

I went with him. He got the kaffirs to inspan the mule-cart, and also to put in a shovel and a pick-axe. All the way to the Mtosa huts Hendrik did not speak. It was a fresh, pleasant morning in spring. The grass everywhere was long and green, and when we got to the higher ground, where the road twists round the krantz, there was still a light mist hanging over the trees. The mules trotted steadily, so that it was a good while before midday when we reached the clump of withaaks that, with their tall, white trunks, stood high above the other thorn-trees. Hendrik stopped the cart. He jumped off and threw the reins to the kaffir in the back seat.

We left the road and followed one of the cow-paths through the bush. After we had gone a few yards we could see the red of the clay huts. But we also saw, on a branch overhanging the footpath, a length of ox-riem, the end of which had been cut. The ox-riem swayed in the wind, and at once, when I saw Hendrik Oberholzer's face, I knew what had happened. After writing the letter to his father Paulus had hanged himself on that branch and the kaffirs had afterwards found him there and had cut him down.

We walked into the circle of huts. The kaffirs lay on the ground under their blankets. But nobody lay in front of that hut where, on that last occasion, I had seen Paulus. Only in front of the door that same kaffir woman was sitting, still stringing white beads on to copper wires. She did not speak when we came up. She just shifted away from the door to let us pass in, and as she moved aside I saw that she was with child.

Inside there was something under a blanket. We knew that it was Paulus. So he lay the day I saw him for the first time with the Mtosas, with the exception that now the blanket was over his head as well. Only his bare toes stuck out underneath the blanket, and on them was red clay that seemed to be freshly dried. Apparently the kaffirs had not found him hanging from the tree until the morning.

Between us we carried the body to the mule-cart.

Then for the first time Hendrik spoke.

"I will not have him back on my farm," he said. "Let him stay out here with the kaffirs. Then he will be near later on, for his child by the kaffir woman to come to him."

But, although Hendrik's voice sounded bitter, there was also sadness in it.

So, by the side of the road to Ramoutsa, amongst the withaaks, we made a grave for Paulus Oberholzer. But the ground was hard. Therefore it was not until late in the afternoon that we had dug a grave deep enough to bury him.

"I knew the Lord would make it right," Hendrik said when we got into the mule-cart.

Karel Flysman

IT was after the English had taken Pretoria that I first met Karel Flysman, Oom Schalk Lourens said.

Karel was about twenty-five. He was a very tall, well-built young man with a red face and curly hair. He was good-looking, and while I was satisfied with what the good Lord had done for me, yet I felt sometimes that if only He had given me a body like what Karel Flysman had got, I would go to church oftener and put more in the collection plate.

When the big commandos broke up, we separated into small companies, so that the English would not be able to catch all the Republican forces at the same time. If we were few and scattered the English would have to look harder to find us in the dongas and bushes and rante. And the English, at the beginning, moved slowly. When their scouts saw us making coffee under the trees by the side of the spruit, where it was cool and pleasant, they turned back to the main army and told their general about us. The general would look through his field-glasses and nod his head a few times.

"Yes," he would say, "that is the enemy. I can see them under those trees. There's that man with the long beard eating out of a pot with his hands. Why doesn't he use a knife and fork? I don't think he can be a gentleman. Bring out the maps and we'll attack them."

Then the general and a few of his kommandants would get together and work it all out.

"This cross I put here will be those trees," the general would say. "This crooked line I am drawing here is the spruit, and this circle will stand for the pot that that man is eating out of with his fingers. . . No, that's no good, now. They've moved the pot. Wonderful how crafty these Boers are."

Anyway, they would work out the plans of our position for half an hour, and at the end of that time they would find out that they had got it all wrong. Because they had been using a map of the Rustenburg District, and actually they were halfway into the Marico. So by the time they had everything ready to attack us, we had already moved off and were making coffee under some other trees.

How do I know all these things? Well, I went right through the Boer

War, and I was only once caught. And that was when our kommandant, Apie Terblanche, led us through the Bushveld by following some maps that he had captured from the British. But Apie Terblanche never was much use. He couldn't even hang a Hottentot properly.

As I was saying, Karel Flysman first joined up with our commando when we were trekking through the Bushveld north of the railway line from Mafeking to Bulawayo. It seemed that he had got separated from his commando and that he had been wandering about through the bush for some days before he came across us. He was mounted on a big black horse and, as he rode well, even for a Boer, he was certainly the finest-looking burgher I had seen for a long time.

One afternoon, when we had been in the saddle since before sunrise, and had also been riding hard the day before, we off-saddled at the foot of a koppie, where the bush was high and thick. We were very tired. A British column had come across us near the Molopo River. The meeting was a surprise for the British as well as for us. We fought for about an hour, but the fire was so heavy that we had to retreat, leaving behind us close on a dozen men, including the veldkornet. Karel Flysman displayed great promptitude and decision. As soon as the first shot was fired he jumped off his horse and threw down his rifle; he crawled away from the enemy on his hands and knees. He crawled very quickly too. An hour later, when we had ourselves given up resisting the English, we came across him in some long grass about a mile away from where the fighting had been. He was still crawling.

Karel Flysman's horse had remained with the rest of the horses, and it was just by good luck that Karel was able to get into the saddle and take to flight with us before the English got too close. We were pursued for a considerable distance. It didn't seem as though we would ever be able to shake off the enemy. I suppose that the reason they followed us so well was because that column could not have been in the charge of a general; their leader must have been only a captain or a kommandant, who probably did not understand how to use a map.

It was towards the afternoon that we discovered that the English were no longer hanging on to our rear. When we dismounted in the thick bush at the foot of the koppie, it was all we could do to unsaddle our horses. Then we lay down on the grass and stretched out our limbs and turned round to get comfortable, but we were so fatigued that it was a long time before we could get into restful positions.

Even then we couldn't get to sleep. The kommandant called us together and selected a number of burghers who were to form a committee to try Karel Flysman for running away. There wasn't much to be said about it. Karel Flysman was young, but at the same time he was old enough to know better. An ordinary burgher has got no right to run away from a fight at the head of the commando. It was the general's place to run away first. As a member of this committee I was at pains to point all this out to the prisoner.

We were seated in a circle on the grass. Karel Flysman stood in the centre. He was bare-headed. His Mauser and bandolier had been taken away from him. His trousers were muddy and broken at the knees from the way in which he had crawled that long distance through the grass. There was also mud on his face. But in spite of all that, there was a fine, manly look about him, and I am sure that others besides myself felt sorry that Karel Flysman should be so much of a coward.

We were sorry for him, in a way. We were also tired, so that we didn't feel like getting up and doing any more shooting. Accordingly we decided that if the kommandant warned him about it we would give him one more chance.

"You have heard what your fellow burghers have decided about you," the kommandant said. "Let this be a lesson to you. A burgher of the Republic who runs away quickly may rise to be kommandant. But a burgher of the Republic must also know that there is a time to fight. And it is better to be shot by the English than by your own people, even though," the kommandant added, "the English can't shoot straight."

So we gave Karel Flysman back his rifle and bandolier, and we went to sleep. We didn't even trouble to put out guards round the camp. It would not have been any use putting out pickets, for they would have been sure to fall asleep, and if the English did come during the night they would know of our whereabouts by falling over our pickets.

As it happened, that night the English came.

The first thing I knew about it was when a man put his foot on my face. He put it on heavily, too, and by the feel of it I could tell that his veldskoens were made of unusually hard ox-hide. In those days, through always being on the alert for the enemy, I was a light sleeper, and that man's boot on my face woke me up without any difficulty. In the darkness I swore at him and he cursed back at me, saying something about the English. So we carried on for a few moments; he spoke about the English; I spoke about my face.

Then I heard the kommandant's voice, shouting out orders for us to stand to arms. I got my rifle and found my way to a sloot where our men were gathering for the fight. Up to that moment it had been too dark for me to distinguish anything that was more than a few feet away from me. But just then the clouds drifted away, and the moon shone down on us. It happened so quickly that for a brief while I was almost afraid. Everything that had been black before suddenly stood out pale and ghostly. The trees became silver with dark shadows in them, and it was amongst these shadows that we strove to see the English. Wherever a branch rustled in the wind or a twig moved, we thought we could see soldiers. Then somebody fired a shot. At once the firing became general.

I had been in many fights before, so that there was nothing new to me in the rattle of Mausers and Lee-Metfords, and in the red spurts of flame that suddenly broke out all round us. We could see little of the English. That meant that they could see even less of us. All we had to aim at were those spurts of flame. We realised quickly that it was only an advance party of the English that we had up against us; it was all rifle fire; the artillery would be coming along behind the main body. What we had to do was to go on shooting a little longer and then slip away before the rest of the English came. Near me a man shouted that he was hit. Many more were hit that night.

I bent down to put another cartridge-clip into my magazine, when I noticed a man lying flat in the sloot, with his arms about his head. His gun lay on the grass in front of him. By his dress and the size of his body I knew it was Karel Flysman. I didn't know whether it was a bullet or cowardice that had brought him down in that way. Therefore, to find out, I trod on his face. He shouted out something about the English, whereupon (as he used the same words), I was satisfied that he was the man who had awakened me with his boot before the fight started. I put some more of my weight on to the foot that was on his face.

"Don't do that. Oh, don't," Karel Flysman shouted. "I am dying. Oh, I am sure I am dying. The English. . . "

I stooped down and examined him. He was unwounded. All that was wrong with him was his spirit.

"God," I said, "why can't you try to be a man, Karel? If you've got to be shot nothing can stop the bullet, whether you are afraid or whether you're not. To see the way you're lying down there anybody would think that you are at least the kommandant-general."

He blurted out a lot of things, but he spoke so rapidly and his lips trembled so much that I couldn't understand much of what he said. And

I didn't want to understand him, either. I kicked him in the ribs and told him to take his rifle and fight, or I would shoot him as he lay. But of course all that was of no use. He was actually so afraid of the enemy that even if he knew for sure that I was going to shoot him he would just have lain down where he was and have waited for the bullet.

In the meantime the fire of the enemy had grown steadier, so that we knew that at any moment we could expect the order to retreat.

"In a few minutes you can get back to your old game of running," I shouted to Karel Flysman, but I don't think he heard much of what I said, on account of the continuous rattle of the rifles.

But he must have heard the word 'running.'

"I can't," he cried. "My legs are too weak. I am dying."

He went on like that some more. He also mentioned a girl's name. He repeated it several times. I think the name was Francina. He shouted out the name and cried out that he didn't want to die. Then a whistle blew, and shortly afterwards we got the order to prepare for the retreat.

I did my best to help Karel out of the sloot. The Englishmen would have laughed if they could have seen that struggle in the moonlight. But the affair didn't last too long. Karel suddenly collapsed back into the sloot and lay still. That time it was a bullet. Karel Flysman was dead.

Often after I have thought of Karel Flysman and of the way he died. I have also thought of that girl he spoke about. Perhaps she thinks of her lover as a hero who laid down his life for his country. And perhaps it is as well that she should think that.

Visitors to Platrand

WHEN Koenrad Wium rode back to his farm at Platrand, in the evening, with fever in his body and blood on his face (Oom Schalk Lourens said), nobody could guess about the sombre thing that was in his heart.

It was easy to guess about the fever, though. For, that night, when he lay on his bed, and the moon shone in through the window, Lettie Wium, his sister, had to shut out the moonlight with a curtain, because of the way that Koenrad kept on trying to rise from the bed in order to blow out the moon.

Koenrad Wium had gone off with Frik Engelbrecht into the Protectorate. They took with them rolls of tobacco and strings of coloured beads, which they were going to barter with the kaffirs for cattle. When he packed his last box of coloured beads on the wagon, Koenrad Wium told me that he and Frik Engelbrecht expected to be away a long time. And I said I supposed they would. That was after I had seen some of the beads.

I knew, then, that Koenrad Wium and Frik Engelbrecht would have to go into the furthest parts of the Protectorate, where only the more ignorant kind of kaffirs are.

Koenrad was very enthusiastic when they set out. But I could see that Frik Engelbrecht was less keen. Frik was courting Koenrad's sister, Lettie. And Lettie's looks were not of the sort that would make a man regard a box of beads as a good enough excuse for departing on a long journey out of the Marico. I felt that his chief reason for going was that he wanted to oblige his future brother-in-law. And this was quite a strange reason.

"The only trouble," Koenrad said, "is that when I get back I'll have to go and live in a bigger district than the Marico. Otherwise I won't have enough space for all my cattle to move about in. The Dwarsberge take up too much room."

But Frik Engelbrecht did not laugh at Koenrad's joke. He only looked sullen.

And I still remember what Lettie answered, when her brother asked her what she would like him to give her for a wedding present, when he had made all that money.

"I would like," Lettie said, after thinking for a few moments, "some beads."

It was singular, therefore, that when Koenrad came back it was without the cattle. And without Frik Engelbrecht. And without the beads.

And he said strange things with the fever on him. He was sick for a long while. And with wasted cheeks, and a hollow look about his eyes, and his forehead bandaged with a white rag, Koenrad Wium lay in bed and talked mad words in his delirium. Consequently, on the days that the lorry from Zeerust came to the post office, there was not the usual crowd of Bushveld farmers discussing the crops and politics. They did not come to the post office anymore: they went, instead, to the farmhouse at Platrand, where they smoked and drank coffee in the bedroom, and listened to Koenrad's babblings.

When the ouderling got to hear about these goings-on, he said it was very scandalous. He said it was a sad thing for the Dopper Church that some of its members could derive amusement from listening to the ravings of a delirious man. The ouderling had a keen sense of duty, and he was not content with merely reprimanding those of his neighbours whom he happened to meet casually. He went straight up to Koenrad's house in Platrand, right into the bedroom, where he found a lot of men sitting around the wall; they were smoking their pipes and occasionally winking at one another.

The ouderling remained there for several hours. He sat very stiffly on a chair near the bed. He glared a good deal at the farmers to show how much he despised them for being so low. And I noticed that the only time his arms were not folded tightly across his chest was when he had one hand up to his ear, owing to the habit that Koenrad had, sometimes, of mumbling. The ouderling was a bit deaf.

And all this time Lettie would pass in and out of the room, silently. She greeted us when we came, and brought us coffee, and said goodbye to us again when we left. But it was hard to gather just exactly what Lettie thought of the daily visits of ours. For she said so little. Just those cool words when we left. And those words, when we came, that we noticed were cooler.

In fact, during the whole period of Koenrad's illness, she spoke on only one other occasion. That was on the third day the ouderling called. And it was to me that she spoke, then.

"I think, Oom Schalk, it is bad for my brother," Lettie said, "if you sit right on top of him, like that. If you can't hear too well what he is saying, you can bend your ear over with your hand, like the ouderling does."

It was hard to follow the drift of Koenrad's remarks. For he kept on bringing in things that he did as a boy. He spoke very much about his childhood days. He told us quite instructive things, too. For instance, we never knew, until then, that Koenrad's father stole. Several times he spoke about his father, and each time he ended up by saying, in a thin sort of voice: "No, father, you must not steal so much. It is not right." He would also say: "You may laugh now, father. But one day you will not laugh."

It was on these occasions that we would look at one another and wink. Sometimes Lettie would come into the room while Koenrad was saying these things about their father. But you could not tell by her face that she heard. There was just that calm and distant look in her eyes.

But we listened most attentively when Koenrad spoke about his trek into the Protectorate with Frik Engelbrecht. He said awful things about thirst and sin and fever, and we held our breath in fear that we should miss a word. It gave me a queer sort of feeling, more than once, to be sitting in that room of sickness, looking at a man with wasted cheeks, whose cracked lips were mumbling dark words. And in the midst of these frightening things he would suddenly talk about little red flowers that lay on the grass. He spoke about the foot of a hill where shadows were. And about small red flowers on the grass. He spoke as though these flowers were the most dreadful part of the story.

It was always at this stage that the argument started amongst the men sitting in the room.

Piet Snyman said it was all nonsense, the first time that Koenrad mentioned the flowers. Piet said that he had never seen any red flowers in the Protectorate, and he had been there often.

Stephanus Naudé agreed with him, and said that Koenrad was just trying to be funny with us, now, and was wasting our time. He said he didn't get up early every morning and ride sixteen miles to hear Koenrad Wium discuss flowers. Piet Snyman sympathised with Stephanus Naudé, and said that he himself had almost as far to ride. "While Koenrad tells us about himself and Engelbrecht, or about his father's dishonesty, we can listen to him," Piet added.

The ouderling held up his hand.

"Broeders," he said. "Let us not judge Koenrad Wium too harshly. Maybe he already had the fever, then, when he thought he saw the red flowers."

Piet Snyman said that was all very well, but then why couldn't Koenrad tell us so, straight out? "After all, we are his guests," Piet explained. "We sit here and drink his coffee, and then he tries to be funny."

There was much that was reasonable in what Piet Snyman said.

We said that Koenrad was not being honest with us, and that it looked as though he had inherited that dishonesty from his father. We said, further, that he wasn't grateful for the trouble we were taking over him. He seemed to forget that it didn't happen to just any sick person to have half the able-bodied men in the Marico watching at his bedside. Practically day and night, you could say. And sitting as near the bed as Lettie would allow us.

Gradually Koenrad began to get better.

But before that happened a kaffir brought a message to us from the man in charge of the Drogevlei post office. The man wanted to know if we would like to have our letters re-addressed to Koenrad Wium's house at Platrand. We realised that it was a sarcastic message, and when we pointed this out to the ouderling, he went to the back of the house and kicked the kaffir for bringing it.

Koenrad's recovery was slow. But when he regained consciousness he did not talk much. Furthermore, he seemed to have no recollection of the things he had said in his days of delirium. He seemed to remember nothing of his mumblings about his boyhood, and about Engelbrecht and the Bechuanaland Protectorate. And although the ouderling questioned him, subtly, when Lettie was in the kitchen and the bedroom door was closed, there was not much that we could learn from his replies.

"Take your father, for instance," the ouderling said – and we looked significantly at one another – "can you remember him in the old days, when you were living in the Cape?"

"Yes," Koenrad answered.

"And did they ever – I mean," the ouderling corrected himself, "did your father ever go away from the house for, say, six months?"

"No," Koenrad replied.

"Twelve months, then?"

"No," Koenrad said.

"Did you ever see him walking about," the ouderling asked, "with a red handkerchief fastened over the lower part of his face?" We could see, from this question, that the ouderling had more exciting ideas than we had about the sort of things that a thief does.

"No," Koenrad said again, looking surprised.

All Koenrad's replies were like that – unsatisfactory. Still, it wasn't the ouderling's fault. We knew that the ouderling had done his best. Piet Snyman's methods, however, were not the same as the ouderling's. His words were not so well thought out.

"You don't seem to remember much about your father – huh?" Piet Snyman said. "But what about all those small red flowers lying around on the grass?"

The change that came over Koenrad Wium's face at this question was astonishing. But he didn't answer. Instead, he drew the blanket over his head and lay very still. Piet Snyman was still trying to pull the blanket off his face, again, when Lettie walked into the bedroom.

"Your brother has had a relapse," the ouderling said to Lettie.

Lettie looked at the ouderling without speaking. She picked up the quinine bottle and knelt at Koenrad's bedside.

Koenrad relapsed quite often after that, when Lettie was in the kitchen. He relapsed four times over questions that the ouderling asked him, and seven times over things that Piet Snyman wanted to know. It was noticeable that Koenrad's condition did not improve very fast.

Nevertheless, his periods of delirium grew fewer, and the number of his visitors dwindled. Towards the end only the ouderling and I were left. And we began discussing, cautiously, the mystery of Frik Engelbrecht's disappearance.

"It's funny about those red flowers on the grass," the ouderling said in a whisper, when Koenrad was asleep. "I wonder if he meant that there was blood on the grass?"

We also said that Lettie seemed to be acting strangely, and I said I wondered how she felt about the fact that her lover had not returned.

"Perhaps she has already got her eye on some other man," the ouderling said, and he pushed out his chest and stroked his beard. "Perhaps what she wants now is an older man, with more understanding. A man who has been married before."

The ouderling was a widower.

I thought he was talking very foolishly. For it was easy to see – from the look of patient dignity that passed over her face whenever she glanced at me – that Lettie preferred the kind of man that I was.

Then, one day, when Koenrad Wium was well enough to be able to move about the room, two men came for him. One wore a policeman's uniform. The other was in plain clothes, and walked with a brisk step. And Lettie opened the door for them and led them into the bedroom, very calmly, as though she had been expecting them.

Marico Moon

BUTTONED up my jacket because of the night wind that came whistling through the thorn-trees (Oom Schalk Lourens said); my fingers on the reins were stiff with the cold.

There were four of us in the mule-cart, driving along the Government Road on our way back from the dance at Withaak. I sat in front with Dirk Prinsloo, a young school-teacher. In the back were Petrus Lemmer and his sister's step-daughter, Annie.

Petrus Lemmer was an elder in the Dutch Reformed Church. He told us that he was very strongly opposed to parties, because people got drunk at parties, and all sorts of improper things happened. He had only gone to the dance at Withaak, he said, because of Annie. He explained that he had to be present to make quite sure that nothing unseemly took place at a dance that his sister's step-daughter went to.

We all thought that it was very fine of Petrus Lemmer to sacrifice his own comfort in that way. And we were very glad when he said that this was one of the most respectable dances he had ever attended.

He said that at two o'clock in the morning. But before that he had said a few other things of so unusual a character that all the women walked out. And they only came back a little later on, after a number of young men had helped Petrus Lemmer out through the front door. One of the young men was Dirk Prinsloo, the school-teacher, and I noticed that there was quite a lot of peach brandy on his clothes. The peach brandy had come out of a big glass that Petrus Lemmer had in his hand, and when he went out of the door he was still saying how glad he was that this was not an improper party, like others he had seen.

Shortly afterwards Petrus Lemmer fell into the dam, backwards. And when they pulled him out he was still holding on to the big glass, very tightly. But when he put the glass to his mouth he said that what was in it tasted to him a lot like water. He threw the glass away, then.

So it came about that, in the early hours of the morning, there were four of us driving along the road back from Withaak. Petrus Lemmer had wanted to stay longer at the dance, after they had pulled him out of the dam and given him a dry pair of trousers and a shirt. But they said, no, it wasn't right that he should go on sacrificing himself like that. Petrus Lemmer said that was nothing. He was willing to sacrifice himself a lot more. He said he would go on sacrificing himself until the morning, if necessary, to make quite sure that nothing disgraceful took place at the dance. But the people said there was no need for him to stay any longer. Nothing more disgraceful could happen than what had already happened, they said.

At first, Petrus Lemmer seemed pleased at what they said. But afterwards he grew a bit more thoughtful. He still appeared to be thinking about it when a number of young men, including Dirk Prinsloo, helped him on to my mule-cart, heavily. His sister's step-daughter, Annie, got into the back seat beside him. Dirk Prinsloo came and sat next to me.

It was a cold night, and the road through the bush was very long. The house where Dirk Prinsloo boarded was the first that we would come to. It was a long way ahead. Then came Petrus Lemmer's farm, several miles further on. I had the longest distance to go of us all.

In between shivering, Petrus Lemmer said how pleased he was that nobody at the dance had used really bad language.

"Nobody except you, Uncle," Annie said then.

Petrus Lemmer explained that anybody was entitled to forget himself a little, after having been thrown into the dam, like he was.

"You weren't thrown, Uncle," Annie said. "You fell in."

"Thrown," Petrus persisted.

"Fell," Annie repeated firmly.

Petrus said that she could have it her way, if she liked. It was no use arguing with a woman, he explained. Women couldn't understand reason, anyway. But what he maintained strongly was that, if you were wet right through, and standing in the cold, you might perhaps say a few things that you wouldn't say ordinarily.

"But even before you fell in the dam, Uncle," Annie went on, "you used bad language. The time all the women walked out. It was awful language. And you said it just for nothing, too. You ought to be ashamed of yourself, Uncle. And you an elder in the Reformed Church."

But Petrus Lemmer said that was different. He said that if he hadn't been at the dance he would like to know what would have happened. That was all he wanted to know. Young girls of today had no sense of gratitude. It was only for Annie's sake that he had come to the dance in the first place. And then they went and threw him into the water.

The moon was big and full above the Dwarsberge; and the wind grew colder; and the stars shone dimly through the thorn-trees that overhung the road.

Then Petrus Lemmer started telling us about other dances he had attended in the Bushveld, long ago. He was a young man, then, he said. And whenever he went to a dance there was a certain amount of trouble. "Just like tonight," he said. He went to lots of dances, and it was always the same thing. They were the scandal of the Marico, those dances he went to. And he said it was no use his exercising his influence, either; people just wouldn't listen to him.

"Influence," Annie said, and I could hear her laughter above the rattling of the mule-cart.

"But there was one dance I went to," Petrus Lemmer continued, "on a farm near Abjaterskop. That was very different. It was a quiet sort of dance. And it was different in every way."

Annie said that perhaps it was different because they didn't have a dam on that farm. But Petrus Lemmer replied, in a cold kind of voice, that he didn't know what Annie was hinting at, and that, anyway, she was old enough to have more sense.

"It was mainly because of Grieta," Petrus Lemmer said, "that I went to that dance at Abjaterskop. And I believed that it was because she hoped to see me there that Grieta went."

Annie said something about this, also. I couldn't hear what it was. But this time Petrus Lemmer ignored her.

"There were not very many people at this dance," he went on. "A large number who had been invited stayed away."

"It seems that other people besides Grieta knew you were going to that dance, Uncle," Annie remarked then.

"It was because of the cold," Petrus Lemmer said shortly. "It was a cold night, just like it is tonight. I wore a new shirt with stripes and I rubbed sheep-fat on my veldskoens, to make them shine. At first I thought it was rather foolish, my taking all this trouble over my appearance, for the sake of a girl whom I had seen only a couple of times. But when I got to the farmhouse at Abjaterskop, where the dance was, and I saw Grieta in the voorkamer, I no longer thought it was foolish of me to get all dressed up like that."

Petrus Lemmer fell silent for a few moments, as though waiting for one of us to say what an interesting story it was, and would he tell us what happened next. But none of us said anything. So Petrus just coughed and went on with his story without being asked. That was the sort of man Petrus Lemmer was.

"I saw Grieta in the voorkamer," Petrus Lemmer repeated, "and she had on a pink frock. She was very pretty. Even now, after all these years, when I look back on it, I can still picture to myself how pretty she was. For a long time I stood at the far end of the room and just watched her. Another young man was wasting her time, talking to her. Afterwards he wasted still more of her time by dancing with her. If it wasn't that I knew that I was the only one in that voorkamer that Grieta cared for, I would have got jealous of the way in which that young fellow carried on. And he kept getting more and more foolish. But afterwards I got tired of standing up against that wall and watching Grieta from a distance. So I sat down on a chair, next to the two men with the guitar and the concertina. For some time I sat and watched Grieta from the chair. By then that fellow was actually wasting her time to the extent of tickling her under the chin with a piece of grass."

Petrus Lemmer stopped talking again, and we listened to the bumping of the mule-cart and the wind in the thorn-trees. The moon was large and full above the Dwarsberge.

"But how did you know that this girl liked you, Oom Petrus?" Dirk Prinsloo asked. It seemed as though the young school-teacher was getting interested in the story.

"Oh, I just knew," Petrus Lemmer replied. "She never said anything to me about it, but with these things you can always tell."

"Yes, I expect you can," Annie said softly, in a far-away sort of voice. And she asked Petrus Lemmer to tell us what happened next.

"It was just like I said it was," Petrus Lemmer continued. "And shortly afterwards Grieta left that foolish young man, with his piece of grass and all, and came past the chair where I was sitting, next to the musicians. She walked past me quickly, and what she said wasn't much above a whisper. But I heard all right. And I didn't even bother to look up and see whether that other fellow had observed anything. I felt so superior to him, at that moment."

Once again Petrus Lemmer paused. But it was obvious that Annie wanted him to get to the end of the story quickly.

"Then did you go and meet Grieta, Oom Petrus?" she asked.

"Oh, yes," Petrus answered. "I was there at the time she said."

"By the third withaak?" Annie asked again. "Under the moon?"

"By the third withaak," Petrus Lemmer replied. "Under the moon."

I wondered how Annie knew all that. In some ways there seemed little that a woman didn't know.

"There's not much more to tell," Petrus Lemmer said. "And I could never unde stand how it happened, either. It was just that, when I met Grieta there, under the thorn-tree, it suddenly seemed that there was nothing I wanted to say to her. And I could see that she felt the same way about it. She seemed just an ordinary woman, like lots of other women. And I felt rather foolish, standing there beside her, wearing a new striped shirt, and with sheep-fat on my veldskoens. And I knew just how she felt, also. At first I tried to pretend to myself that it was the fault of the moon. Then I blamed that fellow with the piece of grass. But I knew all the time that it was nobody's fault. It just happened like that.

"As I have said," Petrus Lemmer concluded sombrely, "I don't know how it came about. And I don't think Grieta knew, either. We stood there wondering – each of us – what it was that had been, a little while before, so attractive about the other. But whatever it was, it had gone. And we both knew that it had gone for good. Then I said that it was getting cold. And Grieta said that perhaps we had better go inside. So we went back to the voorkamer. It seemed an awfully quiet party, and I didn't stay much longer. And I remember how, on my way home, I looked at the moon under which Grieta and I had stood by the thorn-tree. I watched the moon until it went down behind the Dwarsberge."

Petrus Lemmer finished his story, and none of us spoke.

Some distance further on we arrived at the place where Dirk Prinsloo stayed. Dirk got off the mule-cart and said good night. Then he turned to Annie.

"It's funny," he said, "this story of your uncle's. It's queer how things like that happen."

"He's not my uncle," Annie replied. "He's only my stepmother's brother. And I never listen to his stories, anyway."

So we drove on again, the three of us, down the road, through the thorn-trees, with the night wind blowing into our faces. And a little later, when the moon was going down behind the Dwarsberge, it sounded to me as though Annie was crying.

Bushveld Romance

IT'S a queer thing – Oom Schalk Lourens observed – how much trouble people will take to hide their weaknesses from the world. Often, of course, they aren't weaknesses at all; only the people who have these peculiarities don't know that. Another thing they don't know is that the world is aware all the time of these things that they imagine they are concealing. I remember a story my grandfather used to tell of something that happened when he was a boy.

Of course, that was a long time ago. It was before the Great Trek. But it seems that even in those days there was a lot of trouble between the Boers and English. It had a lot to do with slaves. The English Government wanted to free the slaves, my grandfather said, and one man who was very prominent at the meetings that were held to protest against this was Gert van Tonder.

Now, Gert van Tonder was a very able man and a good speaker; he was at his best, too, when dealing with a subject that he knew nothing at all about. He always spoke very loudly then. You can see that he was a fine leader. So, when the slaves were freed and a manifesto was drawn up to be sent to the King of England, the farmers of Graaff-Reinet took it first to Gert van Tonder for his signature.

You can imagine how surprised everybody was when he refused to sign. They didn't know until long afterwards that it was because he couldn't write. He sat with the manifesto in front of him, and the pen in his hand, and said that he had changed his mind. He said that perhaps they were a bit hasty in writing to the King of England about so trivial a matter.

"Even though the slaves are free, now," he said, "it doesn't make a difference. Just let one of my slaves try to act as though he's a free slave, and I'll show him. That's all, just let him try."

The farmers told Gert van Tonder that he was quite right. It didn't really make any difference whether the slaves were free or whether they weren't. But they said that they knew that already. There were a lot of other grievances on the manifesto, they explained, and they were sending it to let the King of England know that unless the Boers got their wrongs redressed they would trek out of Cape Colony.

My grandfather used to say that everybody was still more surprised when Gert van Tonder put down the pen, very firmly, and told the farmers that they could trek right to the other end of Africa, for all he cared. He was quite satisfied with the way the King of England did things, Gert said, and there was a lot about English rule for which they had to be thankful. He said that when he was in Cape Town, some months back, at the Castle, he saw an English soldier leave his post to go and kick a coloured man; he said this gave him a respect for the English that he had never had before. He said that, for somebody who couldn't have been in the country very long, that soldier made an extraordinarily good job of assaulting a coloured person.

The upshot of it all was that, when the farmers of the Cape Colony trekked into the north, with their heavily laden wagons and their long spans of oxen and their guns, Gert van Tonder did not go with them. By that time he was saying that another thing they had to be thankful for was the British navy.

My grandfather often spoke about how small a thing it was that kept Gert van Tonder from being remembered in history as one of the leaders of the nation. And it was all just on account of that one weakness of his – of not wanting people to know that he couldn't read or write.

When I talk of people and their peculiarities it always makes me think of Stoffel Lemmer. He had a weakness that was altogether of a different sort. What was peculiar about Stoffel Lemmer was that if a girl or a woman so much as looked at him he was quite certain that she was in love with him. And what made it worse was that he never had the courage to go up and talk to the girl that he thought was making eyes at him.

Another queer thing about Stoffel Lemmer was that he was just as much in love with the girl as he imagined she was with him. There was that time when that new school-teacher arrived from somewhere in the Cape. The school-teacher we had before that had to leave because he was soft in the head. He was always talking about co-operation between parent and teacher, and he used to encourage the parents to call round at the school building just so that everybody could feel friendly.

At first nobody accepted the invitation: the farmers of Drogevlei were diffident about it, and suspicious. But afterwards one or two of them went, and then more of them, until in the end things got very disgraceful. That was when some of the parents, including Piet Terblans, who had never been to school in his life, started fighting in the classroom over what they should tell the teacher he had to do. Piet Terblans said he had his own ideas about how children should be taught, and he couldn't do his work properly if the other parents kept on interrupting him. He used to drive in to school with the children every morning in the donkey-wagon and he took his lunch with him.

Then one day shortly after the inspector had called the teacher left. Because when the inspector walked into the classroom he found that the teacher wasn't there at all: he had been pulled out into the passage by several of the rougher parents, who were arguing with him about sums. Instead, when the inspector entered the place, two of the parents were busy drawing on the board with coloured chalk, and Piet Terblans was sitting at the desk, looking very solemn and pretending to write things in the register.

They all said that the teacher was quite well educated and gentlemanly, but soft.

So this time the Education Department sent us a woman schoolteacher. Stoffel Lemmer had been at the post office when she arrived. He told me, talking rapidly, that her name was Minnie Bonthuys, and that she had come up from the Cape, and that she had large dark eyes, and that she was in love with him.

"I was standing in the doorway," Stoffel Lemmer explained, "and so it wasn't easy for her to get into the voorkamer. As you know, it is only a small door. She stopped and looked at me without speaking. It was almost as though she looked right through me. She looked me up and down, from my head to my feet, I might say. And then she held her chin up very high. And for that reason I knew that she was in love with me. Every girl that's in love with me looks at me like that. Then she went into the voorkamer sideways, because I was standing in the door; and as she passed she drew her skirts close about her. I expect she was afraid that some of the dust she had on her frock from the motor-lorry might shake off on to my khaki trousers. She was very polite. And the first thing she said when she got inside was that she had heard, in Zeerust, that the Groot Marico is a very good district for pigs."

Stoffel Lemmer went on to say that Piet Terblans, who, out of habit, had again brought his lunch with him, was also there. He said that just before then Piet Terblans had been very busy explaining to the others that he was going to co-operate even more with the new school-teacher than he had done with the last one.

Nevertheless, when the new school-teacher walked into the post office

– Stoffel Lemmer said – Piet Terblans didn't mention anything to her about his ideas on education. Stoffel Lemmer said he didn't know why. It appears that Piet Terblans got as far as clearing his throat several times, as though preparing to introduce himself and his plan to Minnie Bonthuys. But after that he gave it up and ate his lunch instead.

Later on, when I saw the new school-teacher, I was able to understand quite easily why Stoffel Lemmer had fallen in love with her. I could also understand why Piet Terblans didn't manage to interest her very much in the co-operation scheme that had ended up with the previous teacher having to leave the Bushveld. There was no doubt about Minnie Bonthuys being very good-looking, with a lot of black hair that was done up in ringlets. But she had a determined mouth. And in her big dark eyes there was an expression whose meaning was perfectly clear to me. I could see that Minnie Bonthuys knew her own mind and that she was very sure of herself.

As the days passed, Stoffel Lemmer's infatuation for the young school-teacher increased, and he came and spoke to me about it, as was his custom whenever he fancied himself in love with a girl. So I didn't take much notice of the things he said. I had heard them all so often before.

"I saw her again this morning, Oom Schalk," he said to me on one occasion. "I was passing the schoolroom and I was saying her name over to myself, softly. I know I'll never have the courage to go up to her and tell her how I – how I think about her. It's always like that with me, Oom Schalk. I can never bring myself to the point of telling a girl that I love her. Or even saying anything at all to her. I get too frightened somehow. But I saw her this morning, Oom Schalk. I went and leant over the barbed-wire fence, and I saw her standing in front of the window looking out. I saw her quite a while before she saw me, so that by the time she turned her gaze towards me I was leaning more than halfway over the barbed-wire fence."

Stoffel Lemmer shook his head sadly.

"And I could see by that look in her eyes that she loved me, Oom Schalk," he went on, "and by the firm way that her mouth shut when she caught sight of me. In fact, I can hardly even say that she looked at me. It all happened so quickly. She just gave one glance in my direction and then slammed down the window. All girls who are in love with me do just that."

For some moments Stoffel Lemmer remained silent. He seemed to be thinking.

"I would have gone on standing there, Oom Schalk," he ended up in a far-away sort of voice. "Only I couldn't see her anymore, because of the way that the sun was shining on the window-panes. And I only noticed afterwards how much of the barbed wire had been sticking into me."

This is just one example of the sort of thing that Stoffel Lemmer would relate to me, sitting on my stoep. Mostly it was in the evening. And he would look out into the dusk and say that the shadows that lay on the thorn-trees were in his heart also. As I have told you, I had so frequently heard him say exactly the same thing. About other girls.

And always he would end up in the same way – saying what a sorrowful thing it was that he would never be able to tell her how much he loved her. He also said how grateful he was to have somebody who could listen to his sad story with understanding. That one, too, I had heard before. Often.

What's that? Did he ever tell her? Well, I don't know. The last time I saw Stoffel Lemmer was in Zeerust. It was in front of the church, after the ceremony. And by the determined expression that Minnie still had on her face when the wedding guests threw rice and confetti over Stoffel and herself – no, I don't think he ever got up the courage to tell her.

On to Freedom

How we could tell that Gawie Prinsloo had been changed by his experiences on the diggings – Oom Schalk Lourens said – was when he came back from the diamond fields wearing a tie.

It was sad to see a young man altered so much by a few months of pick and shovel work on a claim. We came to the conclusion, however, that it wasn't the time he had spent on his claim with the pick and shovel that had changed Gawie Prinsloo: he must have got changed like that during those periods in which he didn't have a shovel in his hand, and the sweat wasn't dripping off him, and when he wasn't on his claim, even.

And judging by the way he had altered, it would seem that during much of Gawie Prinsloo's stay on the diggings he was not on the claim.

Of course, it was not a new thing in the Bushveld for a young man to go to the diggings, fresh and unspoilt and God-fearing, and to come back different. Often at the Nagmaal the predikant would utter warnings about the dangers of the diamond fields; he would speak in solemn tones about what he called the false glitter of the alluvial diggings, and about the vanity of its carnal shows and sinful worldly riches. But it is just the unfortunate way of the world that many young men, who in the ordinary course would never have thought of leaving the Marico, packed up and went to the diggings after they heard about some of the things the predikant said: about the wild sort of life that was led there, and about the evils of suddenly acquired wealth.

The predikant was on occasion very outspoken in dealing with the shameful things that took place on the diggings, and it was noticeable that at such times certain members of his congregation would shuffle their feet and get restless at his language. And only afterwards the predikant would discover that the reason they were restless was because they wanted to be off to the diggings.

I can still remember a remark that Wynand Oosthuizen once made in regard to this matter. It was when we were preparing to leave Zeerust after the Nagmaal.

"As you all know," Wynand Oosthuizen said, "my farm is situated right up against the Limpopo, and I live there alone. Consequently, I have much time in which to think. And I have thought about this question of the predikant and the young men and the diamond diggings. Yes, I have given it much thought. And I perceive that there is only one way in which the predikant will be able to get people to stay away from the diamond fields: he must say that the diamond fields are a lot like heaven."

We looked at Wynand Oosthuizen, wondering. It seemed to do queer things to a man, living alone like that beside the Limpopo.

Because we made no answer, Wynand Oosthuizen thought, apparently, that we hadn't understood what he was saying.

"You see," he went on, "after every Nagmaal I have observed that there is a big rush to the diamond diggings. That is because the predikant talks so much about the wickedness of the life on the diggings; how the diamond fields are like Babylon, and how vice and evil flourish there, and how people make money there and then forget all about their duty to the church. Now, if the predikant were to say that the diggings are exactly like the Kingdom of Heaven, nobody would want to go. No, nobody at all."

Wynand Oosthuizen winked, then, and set his hat at a slant and strode across to his ox-wagon. In silence, shaking our heads, we watched him getting ready to trek back to the Limpopo.

To do some more thinking, no doubt.

Then there was this matter of Gawie Prinsloo. As I have said, he was more changed than any other man that I had ever seen come back from the diggings. And I had seen many of them come back. Some came back with money that they didn't quite know what to do with: there seemed so much of it. Others came back penniless. One man whom I knew very well was reduced to selling his wagon and oxen on the diggings; and he returned to the Marico on foot, singing.

But Gawie Prinsloo was the only man who had ever come back from the diggings wearing a tie. What was more, it was a red tie; and Gawie Prinsloo said that he was wearing it for a political reason.

It was some time before I realised what Gawie Prinsloo meant by this. Then I proceeded to tell him about politics in the old days. Things were much better then, I said, and much simpler. Politics was concerned only with the question as to which man was going to be president.

"And if the wrong man got elected," I said to Gawie, very pointedly, "you merely inspanned and trekked out of the country. You didn't put on a red tie and walk about talking the sort of thing that you are talking now."

Gawie thought that over for a little while. Then he said that it was cowardly to inspan and trek away from a difficulty. He explained that the right thing to do was to face a problem and to find a solution to it. It was easy to see, he said, how this spirit of trekking away had produced a race of men with weak characters and unenlightened minds.

Naturally, I asked him what he meant by a statement like that. I told him that in the past I had on several occasions trekked out of both the Transvaal and the Free State because I disapproved of the presidents.

"Yes, Oom Schalk," Gawie said, "and look at you."

From that remark, thoughtlessly uttered on a summer afternoon, you can see how much the diggings had altered Gawie Prinsloo.

Afterwards we found out that there were other points about Gawie's new politics besides the wearing of a red tie. For instance, he held views about kaffirs that nobody in the Bushveld had ever heard of before. He spoke a great deal about freedom, and in between mentioning what a good thing freedom was he would mumble something to the effect that in the Marico the kaffirs weren't being treated right.

But, of course, it was quite a while before we discovered the extent to which Gawie Prinsloo's mind had been influenced by this kind of politics. He introduced us to it gradually, as though he was afraid of the shock it might give us if he acquainted us with all his opinions right away.

One day, however, in the home of Jasper Steyn, the ouderling, a number of farmers questioned Gawie Prinsloo closely on his beliefs, and you can imagine the sensation that was caused when he admitted that, in his view, a kaffir was just as good as a white man.

"Do you really mean to say," Jasper Steyn, the ouderling, asked, choosing his words very carefully, "that you can't see any important difference between a kaffir and a white man?"

"No," Gawie Prinsloo answered. "There is only a difference of colour, and that doesn't count."

Several of us burst out laughing at that; the ouderling rocked in his chair from side to side; you could hear him laughing right across in the next district, almost.

"Would you say," the ouderling went on, wiping the tears out of his eyes, "would you say that there was no difference between me and a kaffir? Would you say, for instance, that I am just a white kaffir?"

"Yes," Gawie Prinsloo responded, promptly, "but that's what I thought about you even before I went to the diggings."

Subsequently, others took up the task of questioning Gawie Prinsloo. After he had got over his first sort of diffidence, however, there was no stopping him; he embarked on a long speech about justice and human rights and liberty; and what he kept on stressing all the time was what he called the wrongs to the kaffirs.

It was easy to see that Gawie Prinsloo had been associating with a very questionable type of person on the diggings.

And because we knew that it was the diamond diggings that had led him astray we extended a great deal of tolerance towards his unusual utterances. We treated him as somebody who was not altogether responsible for what he said. In this way it became quite a fashionable pastime in the Marico for people to listen to Gawie Prinsloo talk. And he would talk by the hour about the way the kaffirs were being oppressed.

"Look, Gawie," I said to him once. "Why do you tell only the white people about the injustice that is being inflicted on the kaffirs? Why don't you go and tell the kaffirs about what is being done to them?"

Gawie told me that he had already done so.

"I have gone among the kaffirs," he said, "and I have told them about their wrongs."

But he admitted that his talks didn't seem to do much good, somehow; because the kaffirs just went on smoking dagga – inhaling it through water, he said.

"And when I have told them about their wrongs and about freedom they have laughed," Gawie explained, looking very puzzled. "Loudly."

So the months passed, and Gawie Prinsloo's red tie got crinkled and faded-looking, and when Nagmaal came round again he was still in exactly the same position in regard to his politics; he still spoke fervently about justice for the kaffirs, and he had not yet brought anybody round to his way of thinking. Moreover, he was no longer considered to be amusing. People began to remark that it was annoying to have to listen to his saying the same thing over and over again; they also hinted that it was about time he left the Bushveld.

It was then that Wynand Oosthuizen, once more coming to Zeerust for the Nagmaal, encountered Gawie Prinsloo and his faded red tie and his politics. Several of us were present at this meeting. By this time Gawie Prinsloo was slightly desperate with his message. He had grown so used to people not taking him seriously anymore that he had given up reasoning with them in a calm way. So it was in a markedly aggressive manner that he approached Wynand Oosthuizen.

"The kaffirs," Gawie Prinsloo called out to Wynand, "the kaffirs aren't getting justice in the Marico. And a kaffir is just as good as you are."

Gawie Prinsloo started to walk away, then; but Wynand Oosthuizen pulled him back – by his neck tie.

"Say that again," Wynand demanded.

Nothing if not fearless, Gawie repeated what he had said, and a lot more besides.

Contrary to what we had expected, Wynand Oosthuizen did not get annoyed. Nor did he laugh. Instead, he pushed back his hat and looked intently at the young man with the washed-out red tie.

"This is something new," he said slowly. "I haven't heard that point of view before. And I can't tell whether you are right or wrong. But I have got an idea. My farm is in the far north, on the Limpopo, and I live there alone. I do a lot of thinking there. You come and stay with me until the next Nagmaal, and we will think this question out together."

We were accustomed to Wynand Oosthuizen acting, on occasion, in a singular fashion; it was well known that the loneliness of his life by the Limpopo made his outlook different from that of most people. So we were not surprised at the nature of the invitation that he extended to Gawie Prinsloo. Nor were we surprised at Gawie Prinsloo's acceptance. For that matter, Gawie could not very well have done anything else: Wynand Oosthuizen was holding him so firmly by the tie.

"I will come with you," Gawie Prinsloo said, "but I know that I am right."

Thus it was that they met in Zeerust and arranged to travel together to the Limpopo, to study the new politics about freedom and about equal rights for the kaffirs – Wynand Oosthuizen, the lonely thinker, and Gawie Prinsloo, the young firebrand.

They agreed to meet again in church, at the Nagmaal, and to trek away as soon as possible after the service was over.

And I often wondered, subsequently, to what extent it was the predikant's sermon that had influenced two men who had planned to sojourn by the Limpopo and think of freedom. Because, in the morning, after the Nagmaal service, when Wynand Oosthuizen trekked away in his ox-wagon, Gawie Prinsloo was with him, and together they travelled the long and dusty road that led south, away from the thorn-trees of the Lowveld, to the diggings.

Martha and the Snake

YES, Roderick Guise was his name.
　　I remember the time he first came to live on this side of the Dwarsberge. He came in a donkey-cart and in the back, along with a pile of blankets and things, he had a thick bundle of white paper. We found out at once that he was a man who wrote animal stories. It wasn't difficult for us to find this out, either. For that was the first thing he said to us when he stopped at Kris Lemmer's post office.

"I am Roderick Guise, kêrels," he said. "I am the man who writes the animal stories in the *Huisgenoot* and the *Boereweekblad* and so on. I suppose you have all heard of me."

I could see he was disappointed when we all said that we hadn't heard of him. One man, Martinus Snyman, nearly brought the whole of Drogevlei into disgrace in front of a stranger by thinking that animal stories were stories written by animals. He had seen a horse once in a circus at Zeerust adding up figures, and he thought that perhaps the Englishman had also trained animals to write stories.

Martinus Snyman was easily the most ignorant man I had ever come across.

But afterwards we felt more intimate with this Roderick Guise. By that I mean that we felt less contempt for him. That was after we had found out that Guise was perhaps the Johannesburg way of saying Gous. And at that time Koos Gous was in gaol for smuggling cattle over the Bechuanaland border. So we forgave Roderick Guise for a lot of his nonsense because he had the same name as the biggest cattle-smuggler in the Marico.

Later on, whenever he found two or three of us together, Roderick Guise would take a roll of papers out of his pocket and read us some of his stories. There was one story about a jackal and another one about a lion and quite a few about snakes – mostly rinkhalses and mambas.

What he wrote was all silly stuff. I mean, it might have been true enough for animals that you read about in other countries. Animals like polar bears and whales. But I know that any sensible South African animals would laugh at the nonsense Roderick Guise wrote about what he called Wild Life.

For instance, Guise wrote one story about a leopard chasing him for half a mile across the veld. Now, you know as well as I do that no leopard has ever yet chased a white man, except for fun. And I am sure that particular leopard only chased Roderick so that he could have a story written about him. We, who understand animals, know how vain they can be in that way. And it is just little things like this that people who write about Wild Life will never believe.

But I am sorry that that leopard chased Roderick Guise for only half a mile. While he felt in that playful mood, he should have chased him right out of the Marico District.

One day, when we were sitting in Kris Lemmer's dining room, waiting for the post-cart to bring the letters, a little kaffir-boy came running into the house, shouting that there was a mamba in the Government Road. Lemmer laughed and said that it must be a mamba that had got loose out of one of Roderick Guise's stories.

But we went to have a look.

It was a mamba, all right. When we got into the road we were just in time to see that last few feet of the snake's tail disappearing in the yellow grass.

Kris said that the mamba had come from the direction of the kraal. He suspected that this snake was in the habit of milking one of his cows. Of course, we all know that certain snakes have the habit of getting friendly with a cow and draining her milk. So we told him that was the best way of lying in wait for the snake. Then the post-cart came and we forgot all about it.

Only, I am mentioning this thing about the snake now, because of what happened afterwards. You'll see then that this is a strange story. People who don't know the Marico won't believe this, I suppose. But then, they don't matter. There are always persons like Roderick Guise who tell them lies that they can believe. But I have told you that this is a strange story.

When the predikant came here some years ago, and the ouderling took him aside and told him the whole thing on behalf of the Dwarsberg congregation – for we all decided that it wasn't right for the predikant to hold Nagmaal unless he knew everything – then the predikant turned very pale and trembled a little, and said that the Evil Spirit knows what to make of it.

What we did know was that when he got on to the post-cart, Roderick Guise, the man who wrote animal stories and the man who had vaunted his powers in a cheap and silly way, was the most pitiful spectacle in the whole of the Marico District.

We were all pleased that the arrogance had been taken out of Roderick Guise, and in that way we felt grateful to Martha. By whatever means she had set about making Roderick look the poor creature he really was, she had succeeded remarkably well.

We remembered that in addition to her madness there was another ugly thing about Martha. And that was about the way her mother had died. We wondered how much there was about this that Roderick Guise knew. But, of course, it was useless trying to ask him. He was not in a fit state to talk about that or about anything else. I wonder if he has ever been able to talk again.

Afterwards the kaffirs told us that the Mad White Missus had had a baby. We were surprised about this, in a way. Somehow, from the stories that had grown up around Martha, it did not seem natural to think of her and a baby. In a way, that was about the most terrible thing we had heard about her, so far. You know what I mean. The thought of her baby actually seemed a lot more frightening than her madness, even. We felt that we really had to do something about this.

Then, one morning, a kaffir told us that the baby had died. He didn't know for sure what it had died of, but he believed it was from a snakebite. We all agreed that it was absurd to imagine that a snake would bite a baby that was only a few days old.

It was then that the veldkornet decided that we had to take action.

"This is where the law comes in," he said. "It doesn't matter what else Martha does. But if she has murdered her child the law must have its way."

We agreed with the veldkornet that it was his duty to go over to Martha's farm and make enquiries about the baby's death. But we also made it clear to him that we considered it was his duty to go alone. We could see what he hinted at. He meant that three or four of us should volunteer to go with him. But if he was veldkornet, he should also carry out the duties that went with it, and not drag other people into his affairs.

"If you won't come with me willingly," the veldkornet said, "I shall have to commandeer you."

Accordingly he commandeered four men to go with him. We cleaned and loaded our rifles and early the next morning the five of us set off on horseback. I am sure I never felt more uncomfortable in all my life than I did that morning. And I have been right through the Boer War and I fought with De Wet at Sanna's Post. Yet all those things seemed like nothing at all compared with the heavy feeling I had in my stomach that morning when the five of us were riding down the road together.

By their silence and the expressions on their faces, I could see that my companions felt the same.

Anyway, I'll say no more about this part of the affair, except that we rode twice round the farmyard before going in and we could have gone round a third time if the veldkornet didn't slip off his horse sideways, so that he had to dismount completely to save face. Of course, he said afterwards that he had intended getting off there, anyway, and he had just slipped like that on purpose to dismount more quickly.

Piet Steyn gasped at what we saw then. On the table by the side of the house, in the shade of a big camel-thorn tree, lay the body of a naked baby. I remember the queer, frightened way in which all five of us took off our hats. It must have looked strange to a stranger passing by then to see five armed burghers standing hat in hand and afraid to talk in front of a madwoman's dead baby.

But, of course, nobody could tell from its looks that the mother was mad. It looked just like an ordinary baby, and rather pretty, I thought. And there was no doubt as to how it had died. We had all seen the effects of a mamba's bite and we knew.

The veldkornet whispered to us to return. And we were on the point of going back as noiselessly as we had come, when a queer kind of curiosity made us look through the window. It was what we saw then that made the predikant pray fervently when we told him about it.

What we saw then made us understand a great deal more about what the Bible says of Evil and Sin.

On the bed in front of the window the madwoman Martha was lying. She was awake. Her eyes stared at the ceiling. A long brown mamba lay on her bosom. In what looked like a sweet and soft and very tender way, Martha's hand stroked the head of the snake.

Concertinas and Confetti

Hendrik Uys and I were boys together (Oom Schalk Lourens said). At school we were also classmates. That is, if you can call it being classmates, seeing that our relationship was that we sat together at the same desk, and that Hendrik Uys, who was three years older than I, used to sit almost on top of me so as to make it easier for him to copy off me. And whenever I got an answer wrong Hendrik Uys used to get very annoyed, because it meant that he also got caned for doing bad work, and after we got caned he always used to kick me after we got outside the school.

"This will teach you to pay attention to the teacher when he is talking," Hendrik Uys used to say to me when we were on our way home. "You ought to be ashamed of yourself, when your father is making all these sacrifices to keep you at school. You got two sums wrong, and you made three mistakes in spelling today." And after that he would start kicking me.

And the strange thing is that what he said really made me feel sad, and I felt that in making mistakes in spelling and sums I was throwing away my opportunities; and when he spoke about my father's sacrifices to give me an education I felt that Hendrik Uys was a good son who had fine feelings towards his parents; and it never occurred to me at the time that in not doing any work of his own, but just copying down everything I wrote – that in that respect Hendrik Uys was a lot more ungrateful than I was. In fact, it was only years later that it struck me that in carrying on in the way he was Hendrik Uys was displaying a most unpraiseworthy kind of contempt for his own parents' sacrifices.

And because he spoke so touchingly about my father I had a deep respect for Hendrik Uys. There were no limits to my admiration for him.

Yet afterwards, when I grew up, I found that real life amongst grown-up people was not so very different from what went on in that little schoolroom with the whitewashed walls, and the wooden step that had been worn hollow by the passage of hundreds of little feet – including the somewhat larger veldskoened feet of Hendrik Uys. And the delicate green of the rosyntjie bush that grew just to the side of the school building, within convenient reach of the penknife of the

Hollander schoolmaster, who went out and cut a number of thick but supple canes every morning just after the Bible lesson, before the more strenuous work of the day started.

And I remember how always, after we had been caned for getting wrong answers, Hendrik Uys would walk down the road with me, rubbing the places where the rosyntjie-bush cane had fallen, and calling the schoolmaster a useless, fat-faced, squint-eyed Hollander. But shortly afterwards he would turn on me and upbraid me, and he would say he could not understand how I could have the heart, through my slothfulness, to bring such sorrow to the grey hairs of a poor schoolmaster who already had one foot in the grave.

And as if to emphasise this last statement about its being the schoolmaster's foot that was in the grave, Hendrik Uys would proceed, with each foot alternately, to kick me.

Yes, I suppose you could say that Hendrik was a school-friend of mine.

And once when my father asked him how we got on in school, Hendrik said that it was all right. Only there was rather a lot of copying going on. And he looked meaningly in my direction. Hendrik Uys was so convincing that it was impossible for me to try and tell my father the truth. Instead, I just kept silent and felt very much ashamed of myself. I suppose it is because of what the term 'school-friend' implies that I am glad that our schooling did not last very long in those days.

If he had continued in that way after he had grown up, and had applied to practical life the knowledge of the world which he had acquired in the classroom, there is no doubt that Hendrik Uys would have gone far. I feel sure that he would at least have got elected to the Volksraad.

But when he was a young man something happened to Hendrik Uys that changed him completely. He fell in love with Marie Snyman, and his whole life became different.

I don't think I have ever witnessed so amazing a change in any person as what came over Hendrik Uys in his late twenties when he first discovered that he was in love with Marie Snyman, a dark-haired girl with a low, soft voice and quiet eyes that never seemed to look at you, but that appeared to gaze inwards, always, as though she was looking at frail things. There was a disturbing sort of wisdom in her eyes, shadowy, something like the knowledge that the past has of a future that is made of dust.

"I can't understand how I could have been such a fool," Hendrik Uys said to us one day while we were drinking coffee in the dining room of the new post office. "To think that Marie Snyman was at school with me, and that I never saw her, even, if you know what I mean. She seemed just an ordinary girl to me, with thin legs and her hair in plaits. And she has been living here, in these parts, all these years, and it is only now that I have found her. I wasted all these years when the one woman in my life has been living here, right amongst us, all the time. It seems so foolish, I feel like kicking myself."

When Hendrik Uys spoke those last words about kicking, I moved uneasily on my chair for a moment. Although my schooldays were far in the past, there were still certain painful memories that lingered.

"But I must have been in love with her even then, without knowing it," Hendrik Uys went on, "otherwise I wouldn't have remembered her plaits. Ordinary-looking plaits they seemed, too. Stringy."

"The post-cart with the letters is late," Theunis Bekker said, yawning.

"And her thin legs," Hendrik Uys continued.

"Perhaps the post-cart had trouble getting through the Groen River," Adriaan Schoeman said. "I hear it has been raining in Zeerust."

"Maybe love is like that," Hendrik Uys went on. "It's there a long time, but you don't always know it."

"The post-cart may be stuck in the mud," Theunis Bekker said, yawning again. "The turf beyond Sephton's Nek is all thick, slimy mud when it rains."

"But her eyes weren't like that then, when she was at school," Hendrik Uys finished up lamely. "You know what her eyes are like – quiet, sort of."

His voice trailed off into silence.

And if a great change had come over Hendrik Uys when he fell in love with Marie Snyman, it was nothing compared with the way in which he changed after they were married. For up to that time Hendrik Uys had abundantly fulfilled the promise of his schooldays. He had been appointed a diaken of the Dutch Reformed Church and he was a prominent committee member of the Farmers' Association and the part he was playing in politics was already of such a character as to make more than one person regard him as a prospective candidate for the Volksraad in a few years' time.

And then, I suppose, like every other Volksraad member, he would pay a visit to his old school some day, and he would talk to the teacher and the children and he would tell them that in that same classroom, where the teacher had been a kindly old Hollander, long since dead, the foundation of his public career had been laid. And that he had got into the Volksraad simply through having applied the sound knowledge which he had acquired in the school.

Which would no doubt have been true enough.

But after he had fallen in love with Marie Snyman, Hendrik Uys changed altogether. For one thing, he resigned his position as diaken of the Dutch Reformed Church. This was a shock to everybody, because it was a very honoured position, and many envied him for having received the appointment at so early an age. Then, when he explained the reason for his resignation, the farmers in the neighbourhood were still more shocked.

What Hendrik Uys said was that since he had found Marie Snyman he had been so altered by the purity of her love for him that from now on he wanted to do only honest things. He wanted to be worthy of her love, he said.

"And I used unfair means to get the appointment as diaken," Hendrik Uys explained. "I got it through having induced the predikant to use his influence on my behalf. I had made the predikant a present of two trek-oxen just at that time, when it was uncertain whether the appointment would go to me or to Hans van Tonder."

They were married in the church in Zeerust, Hendrik Uys and Marie Snyman, and that part of the wedding made us feel very uncomfortable, for it was obvious by the sneer that the predikant wore on his face throughout the religious ceremony that he had certain secret reservations about how he thought the marriage was going to turn out. It was obvious that the predikant had been told the reason for Hendrik's resignation as diaken.

But the reception afterwards made up for a lot of the unhappier features of the church ceremony. The guests were seated at long tables in the grounds of the hotel, and when one of the waiters shouted "Aan die brand!" as a signal to the band leader, and the strains of the concertina and the guitars swept across our hearts, thrillingly, like a sudden wind through the grass, and the bride and bridegroom entered, the bride wearing a white satin dress with a long train, and there was confetti in Marie's hair and on Hendrik's shoulders – oh, well, it was all so very beautiful. And it seemed sad that life could not always be like that. It seemed a pity that life was not satisfied to let us always bear on our shoulders things only as light as confetti.

And as a kind of gesture to Hendrik, to let him sort of see that I was prepared to let schooldays be bygones, when the bride and bridegroom drove off on their honeymoon I was the one that flung the old veldskoen after them.

Afterwards, when I was inspanning to go back to the Bushveld, I saw the predikant. I was still thinking about life. By that time I was wondering why it was that we always had to carry in our hearts things that were so much heavier than concertina music borne on the wind. The predikant was talking to a number of Marico farmers grouped around him. And because that sneer was still on his face I could see that the predikant was talking about Hendrik Uys. So I walked nearer.

"He resigned as diaken because he said he bribed me with a couple of trek-oxen," I heard the predikant say. "I wonder what does he take me for? Does he think I am an Evangelist or an Apostolic pastor that I can be bribed with a couple of trek-oxen? And those beasts were as thin as crows. Man, they went for next to nothing on the Johannesburg market."

The men listening to the predikant nodded gravely.

This was the beginning of Hendrik Uys's unpopularity in the Marico Bushveld. It wasn't that Hendrik and Marie were avoided by people, or anything like that: it was just that it came to be recognised that the two of them seemed to prefer to live alone as much as possible. And, of course, there was nothing unfriendly about it all. Only, it seemed strange to me that as long as Hendrik Uys had been cunning and active in pushing his own interests, without being much concerned as to whether the means he employed were right or wrong, he appeared to be generally liked. But when he started becoming honest and over-scrupulous in his dealings with others, then it seemed that people did not have the same kind of affection for him.

I saw less and less of Hendrik and Marie as the years went by. They had a daughter whom they christened Annette. And after that they had no more children. Hendrik made one or two further attempts to get re-appointed as a diaken. He also spoke vaguely of having political ambitions. But it was clear that his heart was no longer in public or social activities. And on those occasions on which I saw him he spoke mostly of his love for his wife, Marie. And he spoke much of how the years had not changed their love. And he said that his greatest desire in life was that his daughter, Annette, should grow up like her mother and make a loyal and gentle and loving wife to a man who would be worthy of her love.

I remembered how Hendrik had spoken about Marie, years before in the post office, when they were first thinking of getting married. And I remembered how he spoke of that stillness that seemed to be so deep a part of her nature. And Hendrik's wife Marie did not seem to change with the passage of the years. She always moved about the house very quietly, and when she spoke it was usually with downcast eyes, and whether she was working, or sitting at rest on the riempies bench, what seemed to come all the time out of her whole personality was a strange and very deep kind of stillness. And the quiet that flowed out of her body did not appear to be like that calmness that comes to one after grief, that tranquillity of the spirit that follows on weeping, but it had in it more of the quality of that other stillness, like when at high noon the veld is still.

I knew that it was this quiet that Hendrik loved above all in his wife Marie, and when he spoke of his daughter Annette – and he spoke of her in such a way that it was clear that he was devoting his whole life to the vision of his daughter growing up to be exactly like her mother – I always knew what that quality was that he looked to find in his daughter, Annette. Even when he never mentioned it in actual words.

Annette grew up to be a very pretty girl, a lot like her mother in looks, and when it came to her turn to be married, it was to Koos de Bruyn, a wealthy farmer from Rustenburg. For her wedding in the church in Zeerust Annette wore the same wedding dress of white satin that her mother had worn twenty years before, and I was surprised to see how little the material had yellowed. It was pleasing to think that there were things that throughout those many years remained unchanged.

And when Annette came out of the church after the ceremony, leaning on her husband's arm, and there was confetti in her hair and on his shoulder, I knew then that it was not only in respect of the white satin dress that there was similarity between the marriage of Annette and that of her mother twenty years before. And I knew that that depth of stillness that Hendrik had loved in his wife would form a part of his daughter's nature, also. And of her life. And for ever. I saw just in a single moment what it was that would bring that stillness of the body and the spirit to Annette for the rest of her married life. And in that way

I guessed what had caused it as well in the case of her mother, Marie, the wife of Hendrik. And I wondered whether Annette's husband would love that quality in her, also.

It was a very slight thing. And it was so very quick that one would hardly have noticed it, even. It was just that something that came into her eyes – so apparently insignificant that it might had been no more than the trembling of an eyelash, almost – when Annette tripped out of the church, leaning on her husband's arm, and she glanced swiftly at a young man with broad shoulders whose very white face was half turned away.

The Story of Hester van Wyk

WHEN I think of the story of Hester van Wyk I often wonder what it is about some stories that I have wanted to tell (Oom Schalk Lourens said). About things that have happened and about people that I have known – and that I still know, some of them; if you can call it knowing a person when your mule-carts pass each other on the Government Road, and you wave your hat cheerfully and call out that it will be a good season for the crops, if only the stalk-borers and other pests keep away, and the other person just nods at you, with a distant sort of a look in his eyes, and says, yes, the Marico Bushveld has unfortunately got more than one kind of pest.

That was what Gawie Steyn said to me one afternoon on the Government Road, when I was on my way to the Drogedal post office for letters and he was on his way home. And it was because of the sorrowful sort of way in which he uttered the word 'unfortunately' that I knew that Gawie Steyn had heard what I had said about him to Frik Prinsloo three weeks before, after the meeting of the Dwarsberg debating society in the schoolroom next to the poort.

In any case, I never finished that story that I told Frik Prinsloo about Gawie Steyn, although I began telling it colourfully enough that night after the meeting of the debating society was over and the farmers and their wives and children had all gone home, and Frik Prinsloo and I were sitting alone on two desks in the middle of the schoolroom, with our feet up, and our pipes pleasantly filled with strong plug-cut tobacco whose thick blue fumes made the school-teacher cough violently at intervals.

The schoolmaster was seated at the table, with his head in his hands, and his face looking very pale in the light of the one paraffin lamp. And he was waiting for us to leave so that he could blow out his lamp and lock up the schoolroom and go home.

The schoolmaster did not interrupt us only with his coughing but also in other ways. For instance, he told us on several occasions that he had a weak chest, and if we had made up our minds to stay on like this in the classroom, talking, after the meeting was over, would we mind very much, he asked, if he opened one of the windows to let out some of the blue clouds of tobacco smoke.

But Frik Prinsloo said that we would mind very much. Not for our sakes, Frik said, but for the schoolmaster's sake. There was nothing worse, Frik explained, than for a man with a weak chest to sit in a room with a window open.

"It is nothing for us," Frik Prinsloo said, "for Schalk Lourens and myself to sit in a room with an open window. We are two Bushveld farmers with sturdy physiques who have been through the Boer War and through the anthrax pestilence. We have survived not only human hardships, but also cattle and sheep and pig diseases. At Magersfontein I even slept in an aardvark hole that was half-full of water with a piece of newspaper tied around my left ankle for the rheumatism. And even so neither Schalk Lourens nor I will be so foolish as to be in a room that has got a window open."

"No," I agreed. "Never."

"And you have to take greater care of your health than any of us," Frik Prinsloo said to the school-teacher. "With your weak chest it would be dangerous for you to have a window open in here. Why, you can't even stand our tobacco smoke. Look at the way you are coughing right now."

After he had knocked the ash out of his pipe into an inkwell that was let into a little round hole in one of the desks, an action which he had performed just in order to show how familiar, for an uneducated man, he was with the ways of a schoolroom, Frik started telling the schoolteacher about other places he had slept in, both during the Boer War and at another time when he was doing transport driving.

Frik Prinsloo embarked on a description of the hardships of a transport driver's life in the old days. It was a story that seemed longer than the most ambitious journey ever undertaken by ox-wagon, and much heavier, and more roundabout. And there was one place where Frik Prinsloo's story got stuck much more hopelessly than any of his oxwagons had ever got stuck in a drift.

Then the schoolmaster said, please, gentlemen, he could not stand it anymore. His health was bad, and while he could perhaps arrange to let us have the use of the schoolroom on some other night, so that I could finish the story that I appeared to be telling to Mr Prinsloo, and he would even provide the paraffin for the lamp himself, he really had to go home and get some sleep.

But Frik Prinsloo said the schoolmaster did not need to worry about the paraffin. We could sit just as comfortably in the dark and talk, he said. For that matter, the schoolmaster could go to sleep in the classroom, if he liked. Just like that, sitting at the table.

"You already look half asleep," Frik told him, winking at me, "and sleeping in a schoolroom is a lot better than what happened to me during the English advance on Bloemfontein, when I slept in a donga with a lot of slime and mud and slippery tadpoles at the bottom. . . "

"In a donga half-full of water with a piece of mealie sacking fastened around your stomach because of the colic," the school-teacher said, speaking with his head still between his hands. "And for heaven's sake, if you have got to sleep out on the veld, why don't you sleep on top of it? Why must you go and lie inside a hole full of water or inside a slimy donga? If you farmers have had hard lives, it seems to me that you yourselves did quite a lot to make them like that."

We ignored this remark of the schoolmaster's, which we both realised was based on his lack of worldly experience, and I went on to relate to Frik Prinsloo those incidents from the life of Gawie Steyn that were responsible for Gawie's talking about Marico pests, some weeks later, in gloomy tones, on the road winding between the thorn-trees to the post office.

And this was one of those stories that I never finished. Because the schoolmaster fell asleep at his table, with the result that he didn't cough anymore, and I could see that because of this Frik Prinsloo could not derive the same amount of amusement from my story. And what is even more strange is that I also found that the funny parts in the story did not sound so funny anymore, now that the schoolmaster was no longer in discomfort. The story seemed to have had much more life in it, somehow, in the earlier stages, when the schoolmaster was anxiously waiting for us to go home, and coughing at intervals through the blue haze of our tobacco smoke.

"And so that man came round again the next night and sang some more songs to Gawie Steyn's wife," I said, "and they were old songs that he sang."

"It sounds to me as though he is even snoring," Frik Prinsloo said. "Imagine that for ill-bred. Here are you telling a story that teaches one all about the true and deep things of life and the schoolmaster is lying with his head on the table, snoring."

"And when Gawie Steyn started objecting after a while," I continued, with a certain amount of difficulty, "the man said the excuse he had to offer was that they were all old songs, anyway, and they didn't mean very much. Old songs had no meaning. They were only dead things from the past. They were yellowed and dust-laden, the man said."

"I've got a good mind to wake him," Frik Prinsloo went on. "First he disturbs us with his coughing and now I can't hear what you're saying because of his snoring. It will be a good thing if we just go home now and leave him. He seems so attached to his old schoolroom. Even staying behind at night to sleep in it. What would people say if I liked ploughing so much that I didn't go home at night, but just lay down and slept on a strip of grass next to a furrow?"

"Then Gawie Steyn said to this man," I continued, with greater difficulty than ever before, "he said that it wasn't so much the old songs he objected to. The old songs might be well enough. But the way his wife listened to the songs, he said, seemed to him to be not so much like an old song as like an old story."

"Not that I don't sleep out on the lands sometimes," Frik Prinsloo explained, "and even in the ploughing season. But then it is the early afternoon of a hot day. And the kaffirs go on with the ploughing all the same. And it is very refreshing, then, to sleep under a withaak tree knowing that the kaffirs are at work in the sun. Sleeping on a strip of green grass next to a furrow. . . "

"Or inside the furrow," the schoolmaster said, and we only noticed then that he was no longer snoring. "Inside a furrow half filled with wet fertiliser and with a turnip fastened on your head because of the blue tongue."

As I have said, this story about Gawie Steyn and his wife is one of those stories that I never finished telling. And I would never have known, either, that Frik Prinsloo had listened to as much of it as I had told him, if it wasn't for Gawie Steyn's manner of greeting me on the Government Road, three weeks later, with sorrowful politeness, like an Englishman.

There is always something unusual about a story that does not come to an end on its own. It is as though that story keeps going on, getting told in a different way each time, as though the story itself is trying to find out what happened next.

It was like the way life came to Hester van Wyk.

Hester was a very pretty girl, with black hair and a way of smiling that seemed very childlike, until you were close enough to her to see what was in her eyes, and then you realised, in that same moment, that no child had ever smiled like that. And whether it was for her black hair or whether it was because of her smile, it so happened that Hester van Wyk was hardly ever without a lover. They came to her, the young men from the neighbourhood. But they also went away again. They tarried for a while, like birds in their passage, and they paid court to her, and sometimes the period in which they wooed her was quite long, and at other times again she would have a lover whose ardour seemed to last for no longer than a few brief weeks before he also went his way.

And it seemed that the story of Hester van Wyk and her lovers was also one of those stories that I have mentioned to you, whose end never gets told.

And Gert van Wyk, Hester's father, would talk to me about these young men that came into his daughter's life. He talked to me both as a neighbour and as a relative on his wife's side, and while what he said to me about Hester and her lovers were mostly words spoken lightly, in the way that you flick a pebble into a dam, and watch the yellow ripples widening, there were also times when he spoke differently. And then what he said was like the way a footsore wanderer flings his pack on to the ground.

"She's a pretty girl," Gert said to me. "Yes, she is pretty enough. But her trouble is that she is too soft-hearted. These young men come to her, and they tell her stories. Sad stories about their lives. And she listens to their stories. And she feels sorry for them. And she says that they must be very nice young men for life to have treated them so badly. She even tries to tell me some of these stories, so that I should also feel sorry for them. But, of course, I have got too much sense to listen. I simply tell her – "

"Yes," I answered, nodding, "you tell her that what the young man says is a lot of lies. And by the time you have convinced her about one lover's lies you find that he has already departed, and that some other young man has got into the habit of coming to your house three times a week, and that he is busy telling her a totally new and different story."

"That's what he imagines," Gert van Wyk replied, "that it's new. But it's always the same old story. Only, instead of telling of his unhappy childhood the new young man will talk about his aged mother, or about how life has been cruel to him, so that he has got to help on the farm, for which he isn't suited at all, because it makes him dizzy to have to pump water out of the borehole for the cattle – up and down, up and down, like that, with the pump-handle – when all the time his real ambition is to have the job of wearing a blue and gold uniform outside of a bioscope in Johannesburg. And my daughter Hester is so soft-hearted that she goes on listening to these same stupid stories day after day, year in and year out."

"Yes," I said, "they are the same old stories."

And I thought of what Gawie Steyn said about the man who sang old songs to his wife. And it seemed that Hester van Wyk's was also an old story, and that for that reason it would never end.

"Did she also have a young man who said that he was not worthy of her because he was not educated?" I asked Gert. "And did she take pity on him because he said people looked down on him because of his table manners?"

"Yes," Gert answered with alacrity, "he said he was badly brought up and always forgot to take the teaspoon out of the cup before drinking his coffee."

"Did she also have a young man who got her sympathy by telling her that he had fallen in love years ago, and that he had lost that girl, because her parents had objected to him, and that he could never fall in love again?"

"Quite right," Gert said. "This young man said that his first girl's parents refused to let her marry him because his forehead was too low. Even though he tried to make it look higher by training his eyebrows down and shaving the hair off most of the top of his head. But how do you know all these things?"

"There are only a few stories that young men tell girls in order to get their sympathy," I said to Gert. "There are only a handful of stories like that. But it seems to me that your daughter Hester has been told them all. And more than once, too, sometimes, by the look of it."

"And you can imagine how awful that young man with the low forehead looked," Gert continued. "He must have been unattractive enough before. But with his eyebrows trained down and the top of his head shaved clean off, he looked more like a – "

"And for that very reason, of course," I explained, "your daughter Hester fell in love with him. After she had heard his story."

And it seemed to me that the oldest story of all must be the story of a woman's heart.

It was some years after this, when Gert van Wyk and his family had moved out of the Marico into the Waterberg, that I heard that Hester van Wyk had married. And I knew then what had happened, of course. And I knew it even without Gert having had to tell me.

I knew then that some young man must have come to Hester van Wyk from out of some far-lying part of the Waterberg. He came to her and found her. And in finding her he had no story to tell.

But what I have no means of telling, now that I have related to you all that I know, is whether this is the end of the story about Hester van Wyk.

The Wind in the Tree

THERE were dark patches on the washed-out blue of Gerrit van Biljon's shirt (Oom Schalk Lourens said), when I saw him on that forenoon, kneeling before a hole that he had been chopping out of the stony ground in front of his house. Those patches were damp marks of sweat. Gerrit van Biljon was kneeling down in front of the hole, on that forenoon of a summer's day when I saw him, and he was scraping out fragments of loosened earth and stones with his hands.

The ground was very hard, and Gerrit was digging the hole with a long cold chisel and a heavy hammer, which were more serviceable than the pick-axe with which he had evidently commenced digging, and which was now lying some distance away from the hole. About twenty yards away, to be exact. It was apparent to me that that was how far Gerrit van Biljon had thrown the pick at the moment when he had decided to go to the tool-shed for the hammer and cold chisel.

"You are digging, Neef Gerrit," I observed.

I was curious why a farmer of the Marico Bushveld should be down on his hands and knees, like the way Gerrit was, in the heat of the forenoon, with the sweat coming out through his shirt in dark patches, and the sun striking on to the back of his neck, in the space between the wide brim of his hat and the top of his faded shirt-collar.

Gerrit van Biljon did not answer. Instead, he reached still deeper into the hole and started feeling for more bits of loose ground. The sun beat full on to the back of his neck, which would have been very red by now if he had been an Englishman. As it was, no amount of sun could do much more to the colour of the back of Gerrit's neck, which was already almost as brown as the earth lying beside the hole. The worst that could happen to Gerrit would be sunstroke. And as you know, the most suitable conditions under which you can get sunstroke in the Marico are when the rays of the midday sun strike on the back of your neck through a thin haze of cloud.

Therefore, when for the second time Gerrit van Biljon had not answered my question, I looked hopefully upwards. But from one horizon to the other the heavens were a deep and intense blue. Bush and koppie, withaak and kremetart and kameeldoring were dreaming languidly under a cloudless sky. I realised that there was not much prospect of Gerrit getting sunstroke, but I nevertheless consoled myself with the thought that having the full blaze on his neck like that must be very unpleasant for him.

I also realised that it was no use my asking Gerrit van Biljon any more direct questions. So I tried sideways, in the manner in which De Wet, after studying the ground, brought his commando round to that part of Sanna's Post where the English general did not want any Mauser bullets to come from.

"Have the Bechuanas on your farm trekked somewhere else, Neef Gerrit?" I asked, casually. "Back to the Protectorate, perhaps?"

Thus I succeeded, for the first time, in getting Gerrit van Biljon to talk.

"No, they have not left," he replied. And then, a little later, after he had struck the cold chisel about another half-dozen times, he asked, very reluctantly, "Why?"

"Because, if the Bechuanas have not left," I answered, "why is it that you, a Marico Boer, should so far have forgotten about farming, as to be here, on your hands and knees, digging a hole in the ground and in the hot sun, with the sweat making all those damp patches on your shirt?"

And after I had looked the back of Gerrit van Biljon over carefully, from his battered hat to his patched veldskoens, I added, "Like a kaffir."

When Gerrit stood up, at that point, and dusted some of the worst pieces of loose earth from the knees of his khaki trousers, I noticed that his digging the hole had not done his hands much good. I don't mean the scraping-out portion of the digging. That part had been all right: his hands were tough enough for that. But I could see that there had been a few occasions when Gerrit had missed the head of the cold chisel. I could see that from his left hand. And it also seemed that he had swung his hammer quite powerfully on those occasions when he had missed.

"I am digging," Gerrit van Biljon said to me, and he spoke with a grave thoughtfulness, as though he wanted to make quite sure that he used the right words, "a hole."

I said that I had thought as much. I told him that I believed that he had first used the pick and had found that it was not much good. And that he had then gone to fetch the cold chisel.

"It doesn't look as though that is much good, either," I added.

Gerrit van Biljon put his left hand behind his back with what he apparently thought was an unobtrusive gesture.

"No," he said, "I am getting on all right."

"And after you have finished digging the hole?" I enquired, trying to sound unconcerned, and as though I was really thinking about something else.

"Then," Gerrit said solemnly, "I am going to dig another hole."

That was how difficult it was for me to find out, on that hot forenoon that was already lengthening into midday, why Gerrit van Biljon was digging holes in the stony ground in front of his house.

So I sat down on the grass under a nearby thorn-tree. I lit my pipe, and while the blue smoke curled away among the green foliage I reflected on the strange way in which the mind of the human being works, and how the human being can always distinguish, very readily, between what is important and what is unimportant. Thus, I had set out from my farm early that morning on foot to search for my mules that had strayed out of the camp two days before. And when in the course of my wanderings through the bush I had at various times come across four kaffirs, each of whom had, in reply to my questionings, pointed in a different direction, I knew that the mules could not be far off. Mules are like that.

But my search for the mules had led me as far as Gerrit van Biljon's homestead, and the moment I saw Gerrit crouched over that hole in the ground I knew right away, without having to think, even, that it was more important for me to satisfy my curiosity in regard to what Gerrit van Biljon was doing than to find the mules. And so I decided to stay.

When the sun was directly overhead Gerrit's wife Sarie came and called us for dinner. Gerrit and Sarie had several young children who would not be back from school until the afternoon. Accordingly, the three of us arranged ourselves about the table in the voorkamer. While we ate we talked at first only of trivial things. I said that what had brought me there was that I was looking for my mules, which had strayed.

"It seems to me that it is not only your mules that have strayed," Gerrit van Biljon said, without looking up from his plate. "If you stay away from your farm much longer it will be your mules that will be starting to look for you."

This remark of Gerrit's made me feel rather uncomfortable. Therefore, to relieve the tension, I began relating what I thought was an amusing little story about Koos Venter, who had at one time farmed at Derdepoort, and who had started digging holes on his farm because of something a kaffir witch-doctor had told him about buried treasure.

"His pick was very blunt by the time they took it away from him," I said. "And when they put him on the lorry for Pretoria, and he was singing, nobody knew for sure whether he was mad before he started digging those holes, or whether he went mad, at a later stage, from sunstroke. But next time you go near Derdepoort you must have a look at that farm where Koos Venter stayed. It has got so many holes in it that the man who is on it now says that he is wondering if he can't use it as some sort of sieve. He thinks the Government might be able to make use of his farm for sifting something in a big way. But he can't think what, exactly. Yes, it is lucky that it does not rain very often in this part of the Marico. Because in wet weather that farm leaks very badly.

"You'll probably be able to see that farm quite soon, now, Neef Gerrit," I finished up significantly. "The lorry for Pretoria passes that way."

I would have said still more. But at that moment I caught Sarie's eye. Gerrit van Biljon's wife Sarie was a pleasant-looking woman. When she smiled her eyes had a pretty trick of getting long and narrow, so that she looked like a little girl, and there came with her smile a soft and alluring curve to her lips. But Sarie's eyes got narrow now in a manner I did not like. And what curves there were on her lips went all the wrong way.

So I said that I was only joking. And that I had best be going. And that I didn't think I would really wait for coffee. And that perhaps the mules were quite near, somewhere, waiting for me, maybe, and that if I didn't leave at once I might miss them.

And so it came about, just because I no longer had any curiosity in that direction, that Gerrit van Biljon explained to me what it was that he was doing. While he talked, his wife Sarie came into the voorkamer several times with coffee. Sometimes she lingered a little while, and I noticed that whenever she glanced in her husband's direction, while he talked, there was a look in her eyes which made me realise what risks I had been running in jesting about Gerrit. And when she walked about the room, driving out the flies with quick little movements, I knew that the cloth she was waving around was not a piece of wedding-dress.

It was a simple story that Gerrit van Biljon told me, and he took a long time over it, and when he had finished with the telling it was no story at all. And that was one of the reasons why I liked his story.

"I am planting bluegum trees," Gerrit van Biljon said, "in those holes that I am digging. For shade."

I was speechless. For a moment I wondered if Gerrit van Biljon's condition was not perhaps even worse than the state of mind of Koos Venter, the other man who had dug holes on his farm.

"But trees," I said, "Neef Gerrit, trees. Surely the whole Marico is full of trees. I mean, there is nothing here but trees. We can't even grow mealies. Why, you had to chop down hundreds of trees to clear a space for your homestead and the cattle-kraal. And they are all shady trees, too."

Gerrit van Biljon shook his head. And he told me the story of how he met his wife Sarie on her father's farm in Schweizer-Reneke, in front of the farmhouse, under a tall bluegum. It was a simple story of a boy and girl who fell in love. Of initials carved on a white tree-trunk. Of a smile in the dusk. And hands touching and a quick kiss. And tears. Oh, it was a very simple story that Gerrit van Biljon told me. And as he spoke I could see that it was a story that would go on for ever. Two lovers in the evening and a pale wind in a tall tree. And Sarie's red lips. And two hearts haunted for ever by the fragrance of the bluegum trees. No, there was nothing at all in that story. It was the sort of thing that happens every day. It was just something foolish about the human heart.

"And if it had been any other but a bluegum tree," Gerrit van Biljon said, "it would not have been the same thing."

I knew better, of course, but I did not tell him so.

Then Gerrit explained that he was going to plant a row of bluegums in front of his house.

"I have ordered the plants from the Government Test Station in Potchefstroom," he went on. "I am getting only the best plants. It takes a bluegum only twelve years to grow to its full height. For the first couple of years the trees will grow hardly at all, because of the stones. But after a few years, when the roots have found their way into the deeper parts of the soil, the trunks will shoot up very quickly. And in the late afternoons I shall sit under the tallest bluegum, with my wife beside me and our children playing about. The wind stirring through a bluegum makes a different sound from when it blows through any other tree. And a bluegum's shadow on the ground has an altogether different feeling from any other kind of shadow. At least, that is how it is for me."

Gerrit van Biljon said he didn't even care if a pig occasionally wandered away from the trough at the back of the house, at feeding time, and scratched himself on the trunk of one of the trees. That was how tolerant the thought of the bluegums made him feel.

"Only," he added, rather quickly, "I only hope the pig doesn't overdo it. I don't want him to make a habit of it, of course.

"Perhaps I will even read a book under one of the trees, some day," Gerrit said, finally. "You see, outside of the Bible I have never read a book. Just bits of newspaper and things. Yes, perhaps I will even read a book. But mostly – well, mostly I will just rest."

So that was Gerrit van Biljon's story.

As he had prophesied, the bluegums, after not seeming to want to grow at all, at first, suddenly started to shoot up, and they grew almost to their full height in something over eight years. And I often saw Sarie sitting under the tallest tree, with her youngest child playing on the grass beside her, and I was sure that Gerrit van Biljon rested as peacefully under the withaak by the foot of the koppie at the far end of the farm as he would have done in the bluegum's shade.

Camp-fires at Nagmaal

OF course, the old days were best (Oom Schalk Lourens said), I mean the really old days. Those times when we still used to pray, "Lord give us food and clothes. The veldskoens we make ourselves."

There was faith in the land in those days. And when things went wrong we used to rely on our own hands and wills, and when we asked for the help of the Lord we also knew the strength of our trek-chains. It was quite a few years before the Boer War that what I can call the old days came to an end. That was when the Boers in these parts stopped making the soles of their veldskoens out of strips of raw leather that they cut from quagga skins. Instead, they started using the new kind of blue sole that came up from the Cape in big square pieces, and that they bought at the Indian store.

I remember the first time I made myself a pair of veldskoens out of that blue sole. The stuff was easy to work with, and smooth. And all the time I was making the veldskoens I knew it was very wrong. And I was still more disappointed when I found that the blue sole wore well. If anything, it was even better than raw quagga hide. This circumstance was very regrettable to me. And there remained something foreign to me about those veldskoens, even after they had served me through two kaffir wars.

It was in the early days, also, that a strange set of circumstances unfolded, in which the lives of three people, Maans Prinsloo and Stoffelina Lemmer and Petrus Steyn, became intertwined like the strands of the grass covers that native women weave for their beer-pots: in some places your eye can separate the various strands of plaited grass, the one from the other; in other places the weaving is all of one piece.

And the story of the lives of these three people, two men and a girl, is something that could only have happened long ago, when there was still faith in the Transvaal, and the stars in the sky were constant, and only the wind changed.

Maans Prinsloo and I were young men together, and I knew Stoffelina Lemmer well, also. But because Petrus Steyn, who was a few years older than we were, lived some distance away, to the north, on the borders of the Bechuanaland Protectorate, I did not see him very often. We met mostly at Nagmaals, and then Petrus Steyn would recount to us, at great length, the things he had seen and the events that had befallen him on his periodic treks into the further parts of the Kalahari Desert.

You can imagine that these stories of Petrus Steyn's were very tedious to listen to. They were empty as the desert is, and as unending. And as flat.

After all, it is easy to understand that Petrus Steyn's visits to the Kalahari Desert would not give him very much to talk about that would be of interest to the listener – no matter how far he trekked. Simply because a desert is a desert. One part of it is exactly like another part. Thousands of square miles of sand dotted with occasional thorn-trees. And a stray buck or two. And, now and again, a few Bushmen who have also strayed – but who don't know it, of course.

I have noticed that Bushmen are always in a hurry. But they have nowhere to go to. Where they are running to is all just desert, like where they came from. So they never know where they are, either. But because they don't care where they are it doesn't matter to them that they are lost. They just don't know any better. All they are concerned about is to keep on hurrying.

Consequently, the stories that Petrus Steyn had to tell of his experiences in the Kalahari Desert were as fatiguing to listen to as if you were actually trekking along with him. And the further he trekked into the desert the more wearisome his narrative became, on account of the interludes getting fewer, there being less buck and less Bushmen the deeper he got into the interior. Even so, we felt that he was keeping on using the same Bushmen over and over again. There was also a small herd of springbok that we were suspicious about in the same way.

You can picture to yourself the scene around one of the fires on the church square in Zeerust. It happened at many Nagmaals. A number of young men and women seated around the fire, and Petrus Steyn, a few years older than the members of his audience, would be talking. And when you saw people's mouths going open, it wasn't in astonishment. They were just yawning.

But there was one reason why the young men and women came to Petrus Steyn, and this reason had nothing to do with his Kalahari stories. But it is one of the things I was thinking about when I spoke about the old days and about the faith that was in the land then. For Petrus Steyn was regarded as a prophet. Sometimes people believed in his prognostications, and sometimes they didn't. But, of course, this made no difference to Petrus Steyn. He didn't care whether or not his prophecies came out. He believed in them just the same. More, even. You would understand what I mean by this if you knew Petrus Steyn.

And Petrus Steyn said that why he went into the Kalahari periodically was in order to get fresh inspiration and guidance in regard to the future. He also said it was written in the Bible that a prophet had to go into the desert.

"I wonder what the Bushmen thought of Zephaniah, when he was in the desert," Maans Prinsloo asked. "I suppose they painted portraits of him, on rocks."

Maans Prinsloo knew that Zephaniah was Petrus Steyn's favourite prophet.

"I don't know whether Ekron was rooted up, like Zephaniah said would happen," Petrus Steyn replied. "I read the Bible right through to Revelations, once, to find out. But I couldn't be sure if Zephaniah was right or not. That's where my prophecies are different. When I see a thing in the Kalahari Desert, that thing comes out, no matter who gets struck down by it" – and Petrus Steyn looked sternly at Maans Prinsloo – "and no matter how long it takes."

That was how Petrus Steyn always talked about his prophecies. And maybe that was the reason why they believed in him, even when they should not have done so.

Anyway, I can still recall, very clearly, that particular Nagmaal at Zeerust when I first understood in which way Stoffelina Lemmer came into the story. And I also knew why. Maans Prinsloo and Petrus Steyn were on unfriendly terms. Stoffelina Lemmer had dark hair, and eyes that had a far-off light in them when she smiled, and that were strangely shadowed when she looked at you without smiling. And she had red lips.

Stoffelina Lemmer was much in Maans Prinsloo's company at this Nagmaal. But she was also a great deal with Petrus Steyn. She was nearly always one of the little group that listened to Petrus Steyn's Kalahari stories, and even if Maans Prinsloo was with her, holding her hand, even, it still seemed that she listened to Petrus Steyn's talk. That is, she appeared, unlike anybody else, actually to listen, and with an interest that was not simulated.

Once or twice, also, after the rest of Petrus Steyn's audience had departed, it was observed that Stoffelina Lemmer remained behind, talking to the prophet. And to judge by the animation of Stoffelina Lemmer's lips and eyes, if they were talking about the future it was not in terms of Petrus Steyn's desert prophecies. Beside the burnt-out camp-fire they lingered thus, once or twice, Stoffelina and Petrus, with the dull glow of the dying embers on their faces.

It was only reasonable, therefore, that Maans Prinsloo should want to know where he stood with Stoffelina Lemmer. That he was in love with her, everybody knew by this time. It was also known, shortly afterwards, that Maans had asked Stoffelina to marry him. And from the way that Maans Prinsloo walked about, looking disconsolate and making remarks of a slighting nature about the whole of the Kalahari, and not just the parts that Petrus Steyn went into, it was clear to us that Stoffelina Lemmer had not accepted Maans Prinsloo just out of hand.

Then, when it was becoming very tense, this situation that involved two men and a girl, Stoffelina Lemmer found a way out.

"Let Petrus Steyn go into the desert again, after this Nagmaal," Stoffelina said. "And let him then come back and tell us what he has seen. He will learn in the Kalahari what is to happen. When he comes back he will tell us."

Although he believed in Petrus Steyn's prophecies, in spite of his pretence to the contrary, Maans Prinsloo nevertheless seemed doubtful.

"But, look," he began, "Petrus Steyn is sure to go in just a little distance. And then he will come out and say that Stoffelina Lemmer is going to marry Petrus Steyn, and that. . . "

Petrus Steyn silenced Maans Prinsloo with a look.

"I shall trek into the Kalahari Desert," he said. "It will be the longest journey I have ever made into the desert. And whatever I see will be prophecy. And just as I see it I shall come back and announce it. Zephaniah may prophesy wrongly, dishonestly, even. . . Petrus Steyn, never! I am still not satisfied about what Zephaniah spoke against Ekron."

Maans Prinsloo was convinced. And so the matter was decided. We inspanned on the Nagmaal plein at Zeerust and journeyed back to our farms by ox-wagon, and shortly afterwards we heard that Petrus Steyn had set out on a long trek into the Kalahari Desert.

Nothing remained to be told after that Nagmaal at which it was decided that Petrus Steyn should trek into the Kalahari once more. The story ended when the last red ember turned to ashes in that camp-fire on the Nagmaal plein.

Maans Prinsloo remained nervous for a very considerable period.

Because this time Petrus Steyn went on a trip that was longer than anything he had ever undertaken before. In fact, he trekked right across the Kalahari, right through to the other side, and far into Portuguese Angola. Indeed, it was more than fifteen years before we again heard of him, and then it was indirectly, through some Boers who had trekked into Portuguese territory in order to get away from British rule.

I often wondered if those Boers had ever asked Petrus Steyn what it was that he had trekked away from.

But before that time there were many Nagmaals, one succeeding the other, when Stoffelina Lemmer and Maans Prinsloo sat near each other, in front of the same camp-fire, each one waiting, and each one's heart crowded with different emotions, for the return of Petrus Steyn from the desert.

No, Stoffelina Lemmer never married Maans Prinsloo.

Seed-time and Harvest

At the time of the big drought (Oom Schalk Lourens said) Jurie Steyn trekked with what was left of his cattle to the Schweizer-Reneke District. His wife, Martha, remained behind on the farm. After a while an ouderling from near Vleisfontein started visiting Jurie Steyn's farm to comfort Martha. And as time went on everybody in the Marico began talking about the ouderling's visits, and they said that the ouderling must be neglecting his own affairs quite a lot, coming to Jurie Steyn's farm so often, especially since Vleisfontein was so far away. Other people, again, said that Vleisfontein couldn't be far enough away for the ouderling: not when Jurie Steyn got back, they said.

The ouderling was a peculiar sort of man, too. When some neighbour called at Jurie Steyn's farm, and Martha was there alone with the ouderling, and the neighbour would drop a hint about the drought breaking some time, meaning that Jurie Steyn would then be coming back to the Marico from the Schweizer-Reneke District with his cattle, then the ouderling would just look very solemn, and he would say that it must be the Lord's will that this drought had descended on the Marico, and that he himself had been as badly stricken by the hand of the Lord as anybody and that the windmill pumped hardly enough water even for his prize Large Whites, and that in spite of what people might think he would be as pleased as anybody else when the rains came again.

That was a long drought. It was a very bitter period. But a good while before the drought broke the ouderling's visits to Martha Steyn had ceased. And the grass was already turning green in the heavy rains that followed on the great drought when Jurie Steyn got back to his farmhouse with his wagon and his red Afrikaner cattle. And by that time the ouderling's visits to Martha were hardly even a memory any longer.

But a while later, when Martha Steyn had a child, again, there was once more a lot of talk, especially among the women. But there was no way of telling how much Jurie Steyn knew or guessed about what was being said about himself and Martha and the ouderling, and about his youngest child, whom they had christened Kobus.

It only seemed that for a good while thereafter Jurie Steyn seemed to be like a man lost in thought. And it would appear that he had grown absent-minded in a way that we hadn't noticed about him before. And it would seem, also, that his absent-mindedness was of a sort that did not make him very reliable in his dealings with his neighbours. It was almost as though what had been happening between the ouderling and Martha Steyn – whatever had been happening – had served to undermine not Martha's moral character but Jurie Steyn's.

This change that had taken place in Jurie Steyn was brought home to me most forcibly some years later in connection with some fence-poles that he had gone to fetch for me from Ramoutsa station. There was a time when I had regarded Jurie Steyn as somebody strong and upright, like a withaak tree, but it seemed that his character had gradually grown flat and twisted along the ground, like the tendrils of a pumpkin that has been planted in the cool side of a manure-pile at the back of the house. And that is a queer thing, too, that I have noticed about pumpkins. They thrive better if you plant them at the back of the house than in the front. Something like that seemed to be the case with Jurie Steyn, too, somehow.

Anyway, it was when the child Kobus was about nine years old, and Jurie Steyn's mind seemed to have grown all curved like a green mamba asleep in the sun, that the incident of the fence-poles occurred.

But I must first tell you about the school-teacher that we had at Drogevlei then. This school-teacher started doing a lot of farming in his spare time. Then he began taking his pupils round to his farm, some afternoons, and he showed them how to plant mealies as part of their school subjects. We all said that that was nonsense, because there was nothing that we couldn't teach the children ourselves, when it came to matters like growing mealies. But the teacher said, no, the children had to learn the theory of what nature did to the seeds, and it was part of natural science studies, and he said our methods of farming were all out of date, anyway.

We didn't know whether our methods of farming were out of date, but we certainly thought that there were things about the teacher's methods of education that were altogether different from anything we had come across so far. Because the school hours got shorter and shorter as the months went by, and the children spent more and more time on the teacher's farm, on their hands and knees, learning how to put things into the ground to make them grow. And when the mealies were about a foot high the teacher made the whole school learn how to pull up the weeds that grew between the mealies. This lesson took about a week: the teacher had planted so large an area. The children would get home from school very tired and stained from their lessons on the red, clayey sort of soil that was on that part of the teacher's farm.

And near the end of the school term, when the dams were drying up, the children were given an examination in pumping water out of the borehole for the teacher's cattle.

But afterwards, when the teacher showed the children how to make a door for his pigsty out of the school blackboard, and how to wrap up his eggs for the Zeerust market in the pages torn from their exercise books, we began wondering whether the more old-fashioned kind of school-teacher was not perhaps better – the kind of schoolmaster who only taught the children to read and write and to do sums, and left the nature-science job of cooking the mangolds for the pigs' supper to the kaffirs.

And then there came that afternoon when I went to see Jurie Steyn about some fence-poles that he had gone to fetch for me from Ramoutsa station, and I found that Jurie was too concerned about something that the teacher had said to be able to pay much attention to my questions. I have mentioned how the deterioration in his moral character took the form of making him absent-minded, at times, in a funny sort of way.

"You can have the next lot I fetch," Jurie said. "I have been so worried about what the school-teacher said that I have already planted all your fence-poles – look, along there – by mistake. I planted them without thinking. I was so concerned about the schoolmaster's impudence that I had got the kaffirs to dig the holes and plant in the poles before I realised what I was doing. But I'll pay you for them, some time – when I get my cheque from the creamery, maybe. And while we are about it, I may as well use up the roll of barbed wire that is also lying at Ramoutsa station, consigned to you. You won't need that barbed wire, now."

"No," I said, looking at my fence-poles planted in a long line. "No, Jurie, I won't need that barbed wire now. And another thing, if you stand here, just to the left of this ant-hill, and you look all along the tops of the poles, you will see that they are not planted in a straight line. You can see the line bends in two places."

But Jurie said, no, he was satisfied with the way he had planted in my fence-poles. The line was straight enough for him, he said. And I felt that this was quite true, and that anything would be straight enough for him – even if it was something as twisted as a raw ox-hide thong that you brei with a stick and a heavy stone slung from a tree.

"What did the school-teacher say about you?" I asked Jurie eventually, doing my best not to let him see how eager I was to hear if what had been said about him was really low enough.

"He said I was dishonest," Jurie answered. "He said. . . "

"How does he know?" I interrupted him quickly. "He's so busy on his farm there, with the harvesting, I didn't think he would have time to hear what is going on among us farmers. Did he make any mention of my fence-poles at all?"

"He didn't mean it that way," Jurie answered, standing to the side of the ant-hill and gazing into the distance with one eye shut. "No, I think those poles are planted in all right. When the schoolmaster told me I was dishonest he meant it in a different sense. But what he said was bad enough. He said that my youngest son, Kobus, was dishonest, and that he feared that in that respect Kobus took after me."

I thought this was very singular. Did not the school-teacher know the story of the ouderling's visits to Jurie Steyn's wife, Martha, in the time of the big drought? Had Jurie Steyn no suspicions, either, about the boy, Kobus, not being his own child? But I did not let on to Jurie Steyn, of course, what my real thoughts were.

"So he said Kobus is dishonest?" I continued, trying to make my voice sound disarming. "Why, did Kobus go along to Ramoutsa station with you, for my poles?"

"No," Jurie Steyn answered. "The schoolmaster won't allow Kobus to stay away from school for a day – not until the harvesting is over. But I am sending Kobus and a kaffir to Ramoutsa on Saturday, by donkey-cart. I am sending him for that roll of barbed wire. And, oh, by the way, Schalk, while Kobus is in Ramoutsa, is there anything you would like him to get for you?"

I thanked Jurie and said, no, there was nothing for me at Ramoutsa that had not already been fetched. Then I asked him another question.

"Did the schoolmaster perhaps say that you and Kobus were a couple of aardvarks?" I asked. "I daresay he used pretty rough language. Snakes, too, he must have said. I mean to say. . . "

"You are quite right," Jurie interrupted me. "That fourth pole from the end must come out. It's not in line."

"The whole lot must come out," I said, "and be planted on my farm. That's what I ordered those poles for."

"That fourth pole of yours, Oom Schalk," Jurie repeated, "must be taken out and planted further to the left – I planted it in crooked because I was so upset by the schoolmaster. It was only when I got home that I realised the cheek of the whole thing. I have got a good mind to report the schoolmaster to the Education Department for writing private letters with school ink. I'd like to see him get out of that one."

If the Education Department did not take any action after the schoolmaster had used the front part of the school building to store his sweet-potatoes in, I did not think they would worry much about this complaint of Jurie Steyn's. By way of explanation the school-teacher told the parents that why he had to store the sweet-potatoes in that part of the school building for a while was because the prices on the Johannesburg market were so low, it was sheer robbery. He also complained that the Johannesburg produce agents had no sense of responsibility in regard to the interests of the farmers.

"If I had so little sense of responsibility about my duties as a school-teacher," he said, "the Education Department would have sacked me long ago."

When the schoolmaster made this remark several of the parents looked at him with a good deal of amazement.

These were the things that were passing through my mind while Jurie Steyn was telling me about the way the school-teacher had insulted him. I was anxious to learn more about it. I tried another way of getting Jurie to talk. I wanted to find out how much the schoolmaster knew, and how much Jurie himself suspected, of the facts of Kobus's paternity. I felt almost as inquisitive as a woman, then.

"I once heard the schoolmaster using very strong expressions, Jurie," I said, "and that was when he spoke to a Pondo kaffir whom he had caught stealing one of the back wheels of his ox-wagon. I have never been able to understand how that kaffir got the wheel off so quickly, because he didn't have a jack, as far as I know, and they say that the wagon had not been outspanned for more than two hours. But that was only a Pondo kaffir without much understanding of the white man's language of abuse. No doubt what the school-teacher said about you and your son Kobus was. . . "

"It's possible to get a back wheel off an ox-wagon even if you haven't got a jack, so long as the wagon isn't too heavily loaded," Jurie said, without giving me a chance to finish, "and as long as you have got two other men to help you. Still, it would be interesting to know how the Pondo did it. Was it dark at the time, do you know?"

I couldn't tell him. But it was getting dark on Jurie Steyn's farm. The deep shadows of the evening lay heavy across the thorn-bushes, and the furthest of my fence-poles had grown blurred against the sky. It seemed a strange thought to me that my fence-poles were that night for the first time standing upright and in silence, like the trees, awaiting the arrival of the first stars.

Jurie Steyn and I started walking towards the farmhouse, in front of which I had left my mule-cart. The boy Kobus came out to meet us, and I could see from the reddish clay on his knees that he had studied hard at school that day.

"You look tired, Kobus," Jurie Steyn said. And his voice suddenly sounded very soft when he spoke.

And in the dusk I saw the way that Kobus's eyes lit up when he took Jurie Steyn's hand. A singular variety of ideas passed through my mind, then, and I found that I no longer bore Jurie Steyn that same measure of resentment on account of his thoughtless way of acting with my fence-poles. I somehow felt that there were more important things in life than the question of what happened to my roll of barbed wire at Ramoutsa. And more important things than what had happened about the ouderling from near Vleisfontein.

The Ghost at the Drift

GHOST stories that I have heard people tell (Oom Schalk Lourens said), are always about the same sort of thing. You must have heard this kind of story often. A traveller is on his way somewhere, and he has to cross a drift after nightfall. People in the neighbourhood warn him that no man has ever been able to ride his horse past the drift in the dark. But the stranger proceeds on his way until he reaches a spot where his horse suddenly rears up in terror. Thereupon the traveller returns to the people who warned him about the drift; and he spends the night with them, and they enlighten him at considerable length about the circumstances of the murder that was committed there long ago, and about the ghost that haunts the place near the drift where the grass does not grow.

This is quite a good story, of course, if it is properly told, without too much detail. You spoil the story if you describe too fully how the ghost looks, and if you try to imitate the noises it makes – as I have heard some storytellers do.

Anyway, I have heard this story so often that I have almost come to the conclusion that there is only one ghost in the Transvaal. And that there has been only one murder.

All this reminds me of the time when Gert Bekker and I were driving by mule-cart to the Kalahari. We went through Rooikrans. Because this was my first visit to the Molopo area, and because Gert Bekker had been on that road before, a singular thing happened to Gert Bekker. He felt that he had to take the lead in everything, and he gave me a lot of instructions and good counsel. Although I had grown up in the Bushveld, Gert Bekker treated me as though I was some newcomer from an overseas city, just because I had not been in that small part of the Groot Marico before – whereas I knew the rest of the district as well as I knew my own farm.

"There are many ways in which a stranger to these parts can deceive himself, Schalk," Gert Bekker was saying. "That kwê-bird that you heard calling now. You thought that sound came from in front, didn't you?"

"I *saw* the kwê-bird when we passed him a few moments ago," I answered. "He was perched on a bough of one of those withaaks to the left there."

"It's a good thing you saw him, then," Gert Bekker continued. "Otherwise you might have got startled. I've seen strangers to these parts – "

"Kwê – ê – ê!" we heard the bird call again.

And so Gert Bekker went on talking, with the mule-cart bumping over the dusty road in the heat of the afternoon. Gert Bekker's voice sounded as empty as the mule-cart's rattling: his conversation was as dusty as the road: I only thought that his words couldn't take a turn as neatly as the cart-wheels did in the sand.

Afterwards, in treating me as a foreigner in the Marico, Gert Bekker even went so far as to begin thinking out lies to tell me. The kind of lies that Marico farmers make up for a stranger from the city, so that they can laugh about it afterwards when they think of how the stranger's jaw fell.

Among other things, Gert Bekker told me of a farmer near the Molopo who had trained a team of green mambas to form themselves into a long chain to draw water from the well in a bucket. "A mamba-chain is no stronger than its weakest link," Gert Bekker said, making up more lies as we went along. And he looked at me sideways, at intervals, to see if my mouth was also beginning to open in astonishment.

Later in the afternoon we outspanned at the farmhouse of Jurie Snyman, whom I had met once or twice in Zeerust at the Nagmaal. I was glad that I could shake hands with Jurie Snyman and say, "Middag, Neef Jurie," quickly, before Gert Bekker could introduce me as "Schalk Lourens, a stranger to these parts" – as he had done at other farmhouses where we had called along the road.

Jurie Snyman's wife brought us coffee into the voorkamer, and we sat and spoke about the new kind of bot-fly pest that was invading the Marico from the Kalahari side.

"Do you know what a bot-fly is, Schalk?" Gert Bekker had the impudence to ask me, still keeping on with his role of being a mentor to a new arrival in that region.

"Yes," I answered, shortly, "and I also know what a pest is."

Jurie Snyman laughed, thinking that I was referring to our Volksraad member who was sitting in Pretoria and had done nothing to get government assistance for the farmers in our struggle against the bot-fly plague. The result was that we spent several hours in discussing our Volksraad member, whom we ended up by talking about as our bot-fly member, so that it was quite late in the afternoon when we again stood beside the mule-cart, which Jurie Snyman's kaffirs were busy inspanning. Jurie Snyman came out with us. His farmhouse faced on to the road. Opposite the farmhouse was a rondavel that was used as a post office. Further down the road, partly hidden by the thorn-trees, was the thatched roof of a schoolroom.

"Your farm is growing into a fair-sized town," Gert Bekker said to Jurie Snyman.

"Yes, indeed," Jurie Snyman answered, proudly. "About half a mile beyond the school building there is also Ouma Theron's house: she's the local midwife. And just behind the bult is the new Indian store. That means five buildings by the road – two on the other side of the road, and three on this side – in a distance of a little more than a mile. There are seventeen pupils in the school. The teacher boards with Haasbroek near the Molopo drift and comes in every day by the donkey-wagon that the Education Department provides for the schoolchildren. My farm is actually the biggest town in the Marico, north of the Dwarsberge, when the school is in session."

Gert Bekker looked at me significantly. He meant that here was something else of which I, a stranger to these parts, had until that moment been ignorant.

We were already seated on the mule-cart when it seemed as though Jurie Snyman had suddenly remembered something. He looked at the sun, which was within an hour of setting.

"You may as well spend the night with me," he said to Gert Bekker. "No man can drive his trek-animals past a certain spot near the Molopo drift after dark. The Molopo is nearly eight miles from here. You won't make it before nightfall."

Gert Bekker, unlike myself, did not guess what was coming. So he said, no, while he was grateful for Jurie Snyman's offer of hospitality, we had arranged to stay over with Faan Cronjé, who lived just across the drift. Faan was his wife's sister-in-law's second cousin on the Liebenberg side, Gert Bekker explained, and he dared not be neglectful of the social obligations when it came to the more intimate kind of family ties.

"But after your mules get a fright there, just before the drift, and they won't go any further," Jurie Snyman said, "then don't sleep out on the veld, but come back here. I'll be expecting you in any case."

Gert Bekker, not guessing what it was all about, looked at Jurie Snyman in some surprise. So I was glad that I was at last presented with an opportunity for enlightening Gert Bekker, instead of having had, until now, to receive all kinds of unwanted information and advice from him. For although I might be a stranger to that small part of the Marico around the Molopo, I was not a foreigner when it came to recognising a story, and in the few remarks that Jurie Snyman had made I detected all the signs of the Transvaal's oldest and most worn kind of ghost story.

"The ghost of a tall woman dressed all in white haunts a spot near the drift," I announced, "and no horse will go past that spot at night."

"And she carries a baby at her breast, and the baby cries," Jurie Snyman added.

"And no grass grows there," I said.

"And around the woman's waist is a long black girdle whose ends reach almost to the ground," Jurie Snyman said again.

At last Gert Bekker was able to find words.

"But how do you know all these things?" he called out to me in astonishment. "I thought you were a strange– "

"It's all to do with a murder of long ago," I replied airily. "Shake the reins."

Before he realised that he was taking instructions from me, Gert Bekker had cracked his whip and the mule-cart began to move off along the road. He waved goodbye to Jurie Snyman.

"You'll be back here this same night," was the last thing we heard Jurie Snyman shout.

There was something in Jurie Snyman's tones that made the afternoon seem later than it already was.

We had driven past the school building and the thatched roof, and past the house of Ouma Theron, the midwife, and past the new Indian store that was about half a mile around the bend, before Gert Bekker again spoke to me. And then I thought that I noticed in his voice a certain measure of respect that had not been there before.

"I suppose it is – it's all just nonsense, Schalk, about – about that woman in the white dress?" Gert Bekker asked me. "And do you think it really is a white dress, or is it just that all ghosts look white?"

"I am sure I don't know," I answered. "I don't know these parts around the Molopo at all. You know what it is when one is a stranger to a place. I thought you were familiar with – "

"I didn't know *all that*," Gert Bekker answered. "And do you think that a murder really was committed there?"

I told him that I didn't know about that, either. I had merely guessed.

"We should have asked Jurie Snyman more about it," Gert Bekker said, "before we drove off in such a hurry. We can't just go by guesswork in a thing like this. When it comes to ghosts you've got to have hard facts. Like how the ghost looks, and everything."

Afterwards, when the shadows began to lengthen, I also started feeling that it would perhaps have been as well if we had asked Jurie Snyman a few more questions. . .

A little further on Gert Bekker again broke the silence.

"Perhaps we don't need to go all that way, across the drift, to spend the night with my wife's relatives," he said. "We can call on them in the morning. I sometimes think that we Afrikaners lay too much stress on family attachments. It is something that becomes unhealthy if it gets overdone. We can perhaps just camp out next to the road, this side of the drift."

"Even a good distance this side of the drift will do," I answered.

"I've got some mealie-meal and coffee and boerewors in the back of the cart," Gert Bekker said again.

"And we can scoop up water out of the next jackal-hole we come to," I said.

We also said that it would be a good idea to pitch camp while there was still plenty of daylight. We would be able to get together a large quantity of dry branches for the fire.

"And a couple of dead tree-trunks," Gert Bekker supplemented. "A dead tree-trunk, if it's a good one, keeps burning all night."

I did not care for the thoughtless way in which Gert Bekker kept on repeating the word 'dead.'

After we had eaten the boerewors and drunk our coffee, and had tethered the mules, we crept in under our blankets beside the fire. I wanted to talk about the thing that was uppermost in my mind, but I could sense that Gert Bekker was afraid to talk about it, and that made me also afraid to broach the subject. It is a peculiar thing that when you are alone at night in the company of a person with an ignorant mind, your own sensible outlook becomes clouded by the other person's superstitions. That was what I felt was happening to me, lying there in the night with Gert Bekker only a few yards away from me.

And, of course – as I learnt afterwards – when Gert Bekker spoke about that night, he always said that if it hadn't been for my absurd kaffir beliefs, which gradually undermined his own sound understanding and education, he would not have been afraid to sleep right next to the drift, on that very spot, even, where the grass did not grow. He didn't mind sleeping on the hard ground, he said.

I mention all this so that you can see from it what an impossible sort of person Gert Bekker always was.

Anyway, we couldn't sleep. We talked about things in which neither of us was at all interested. And we did not speak much above a whisper.

I can't remember when it was that I first sensed something. I turned my head to one side and what I saw then made me dart one swift glance at Gert Bekker, to find out if he had also seen it. I concluded that he had. Because in a single wild movement he pulled the blankets right over his head. I didn't see what he did after that, because at almost the same time I pulled the blankets over my head as well. After all – as Gert Bekker had taken so much care to point out to me – I was a stranger, comparatively speaking, to the Molopo area, and I could therefore do no better, in an emergency of this nature, than to follow his example. He had been on the road to the Molopo before, and he would naturally know that the right thing to do, when you get a sudden glimpse of a spectral shape a few feet away from you – a woman all in white and with the firelight flickering on her ghostly features, and on the child held in her arms – is to pull the blankets over your head very quickly.

I lay a long time in the dark, too frightened to move. The blankets pressed close around my face, but I knew that I wouldn't suffocate: I was afraid to breathe much, in any case. And I knew only one thing, and that was that nothing on earth would induce me to gaze voluntarily upon that ghostly shape again.

I hadn't looked, either, to see if she was wearing a black sash reaching to her feet. . .

I only felt that we had pitched our camp much too near to the drift, after all.

For a long time I heard nothing but the beating of my own heart. I lay like that for hours, it seemed. Then, through the padding of the blankets, I thought I heard – laughter. I listened. No, I couldn't be mistaken. It was, indeed, laughter of a sort. I would know the sound of Gert Bekker's empty guffaws anywhere.

The explanation was simple enough. The wife of Piet Haasbroek was in labour. Piet Haasbroek had left for Rustenburg a few days before by donkey-cart, the family's only form of conveyance. And since there was no one else to send, Rena van Dam, the young school-teacher who boarded with the Haasbroeks, had set out in the dark to call on Ouma Theron, the midwife, whose house we had passed in the afternoon. Rena van Dam had seen the camp-fire and had walked up to get our help.

The mules were quickly inspanned and the three of us drove off to fetch Ouma Theron. An hour or so later the midwife alighted from the mule-cart in front of the Haasbroek home. Gert Bekker and I helped in the kitchen, keeping the fire going for hot water. We also sat around in the voorkamer and smoked.

About all of this, however, there still remained one thing that puzzled me – and it was something that I was shy to ask about. I was on the point of mentioning the matter to Gert Bekker on a few occasions, when we were alone together in the voorkamer and the three women were in the bedroom. And for the reasons I have already given you – to do with Gert Bekker's gross superstitions – I each time restrained myself. And I had the peculiar feeling that Gert Bekker wanted to ask the same question of me, but that something that was almost like fear was holding him back, also.

Round about midnight Mevrou Haasbroek's child was born. Of course, Gert Bekker and I asked to be allowed to see the baby. And, somehow, it seemed to me that the birth of a child in that house, a little while before, and the murder at the drift, long ago, were in that moment equally lonely and solemn things.

We heard voices in the bedroom, and few minutes later Rena van Dam came out, carrying the child wrapped in swaddling-clothes.

And this shows you what a strange thing the imagination is.

For when Gert Bekker spoke then, he uttered the very words that I wanted to say. And he brought up just that thing that I had been worrying about all night.

"That's like the child you had in your arms when I first saw you by the camp-fire," Gert Bekker exclaimed, "before I pulled the blankets over my head."

From her answer, it appeared to me that Rena van Dam had been a school-teacher in the Molopo area somewhat too long. It must be the influence of the neighbourhood that affected her, I decided. And I felt sad to think that an educated girl should suffer like that from self-delusions.

"When *I* got to the camp-fire," Rena van Dam said, "you were both of you already lying with your heads under the blankets. I saw the two of you by the light of the fire when I was still a long way off."

Dopper and Papist

It was a cold night (Oom Schalk Lourens said) on which we drove with Gert Bekker in his Cape-cart to Zeerust. I sat in front, next to Gert, who was driving. In the back seat were the predikant, Rev. Vermooten, and his ouderling, Isak Erasmus, who were on their way to Pretoria for the meeting of the synod of the Dutch Reformed Church. The predikant was lean and hawk-faced; the ouderling was fat and had broad shoulders.

Gert Bekker and I did not speak. We had been transport drivers together in our time, and we had learnt that when it is two men alone, travelling over a long distance, it is best to use few words, and those well chosen. Two men, alone in each other's company, understand each other better the less they speak.

The horses kept up a good, steady trot. The lantern, swinging from side to side with the jogging of the cart, lit up stray patches of the uneven road and made bulky shadows rise up among the thorn-trees. In the back seat the predikant and the ouderling were discussing theology.

"You never saw such a lot of brandsiek sheep in your life," the predikant was saying, "as what Chris Haasbroek brought along as tithe."

We then came to a stony part of the road, and so I did not hear the ouderling's reply; but afterwards, above the rattling of the cart-wheels, I caught other snatches of God-fearing conversation, to do with the raising of pew-rents.

From there the predikant started discussing the proselytising activities being carried on among the local Bapedi kaffirs by the Catholic mission at Vleisfontein. The predikant dwelt particularly on the ignorance of the Bapedi tribes and on the idolatrous form of the Papist communion service, which was quite different from the Protestant Nagmaal, the predikant said, although to a Bapedi, walking with his buttocks sticking out, the two services might, perhaps, seem somewhat alike.

Rev. Vermooten was very eloquent when he came to denouncing the heresies of Catholicism. And he spoke loudly, so that we could hear him on the front seat. And I know that both Gert Bekker and I felt very good, then, deep inside us, to think that we were Protestants. The coldness of the night and the pale flickering of the lantern-light among the thorn-trees gave an added solemnity to the predikant's words.

I felt that it might perhaps be all right to be a Catholic if you were walking on the Zeerust sidewalk in broad daylight, say. But it was a different matter to be driving through the middle of the bush on a dark night, with just a swinging lantern fastened to the side of a Cape-cart with baling-wire. If the lantern went out suddenly, and you were left in the loneliest part of the bush, striking matches, then it must be a very frightening thing to be a Catholic, I thought.

This led me to thinking of Piet Reilly and his family, who were Afrikaners, like you and me, except that they were Catholics. Piet Reilly even brought out his vote for General Lemmer at the last Volksraad election, which we thought would make it unlucky for our candidate. But General Lemmer said, no, he didn't mind how many Catholics voted for him. A Catholic's vote was, naturally, not as good as a Dopper's, he said, but the little cross that had to be made behind a candidate's name cast out the evil that was of course otherwise lurking in a Catholic's ballot paper. And General Lemmer must have been right, because he got elected, that time.

While I was thinking on these lines, it suddenly struck me that Piet Reilly was now living on a farm about six miles on the Bushveld side of Sephton's Nek, and that we would be passing his farmhouse, which was near the road, just before daybreak. It was comforting to think that we would have the predikant and the ouderling in the Cape-cart with us, when we passed the homestead of Piet Reilly, a Catholic, in the dark.

I tried to hear what the predikant was saying, in the back seat, to the ouderling. But the predikant was once more dealing with an abstruse point of religion, and had lowered his voice accordingly. I could catch only fragments of the ouderling's replies.

"Yes, dominee," I heard the ouderling affirm, "you are quite right. If he again tries to overlook your son for the job of anthrax inspector, then you must make it clear to the Chairman of the Board that you have all that information about his private life. . . "

I realised then that you could find much useful guidance for your everyday problems in the conversation of holy men.

The night got colder and darker.

The palm of my hand, pressed tight around the bowl of my pipe, was the only part of me that felt warm. My teeth began to chatter. I wished that, next time we stopped to let the horses blow, we could light a fire and boil coffee. But I knew that there was no coffee left in the chest under the back seat.

While I sat silent next to Gert Bekker, I continued to think of Piet Reilly and his wife and children. With Piet, of course, I could understand it. He himself had merely kept up the religion – if you can call what the Catholics believe in a religion – that he had inherited from his father and his grandfather. But there was Piet Reilly's wife, Gertruida, now. She had been brought up a respectable Dopper girl. She was one of the Drogedal Bekkers, and was, in fact, distantly related to Gert Bekker, who was sitting on the Cape-cart next to me. There was something for you to ponder about, I thought to myself, with the cold all the time looking for new places in my skin through which to strike into my bones.

The moment Gertruida met Piet Reilly she forgot all about the sacred truths she had learnt at her mother's knee. And on the day she got married she was saying prayers to the Virgin Mary on a string of beads, and was wearing a silver cross at her throat that was as soft and white as the roses she held pressed against her. Here was now a sweet Dopper girl turned Papist.

As I have said, I knew that there was no coffee left in the box under the back seat; but I did know that under the front seat there was a full bottle of raw peach brandy. In fact, I could see the neck of the bottle protruding from between Gert Bekker's ankles.

I also knew, through all the years of transport driving that we had done together, that Gert Bekker had already, over many miles of road, been thinking how we could get the cork off the bottle without the predikant and the ouderling shaking their heads reprovingly. And the way he managed it in the end was, I thought, highly intelligent.

For, when he stopped the cart again to rest the horses, he alighted beside the road and held out the bottle to our full view.

"There is brandy in this bottle, dominee," Gert Bekker said to the predikant, "that I keep for the sake of the horses on cold nights, like now. It is an old Marico remedy for when the horses are in danger of getting the floute. I take a few mouthfuls of the brandy, which I then blow into the nostrils of the horses, who don't feel the cold so much, after that. The brandy revives them."

Gert commenced blowing brandy into the face of the horse on the near side, to show us.

Then he beckoned to me, and I also alighted and went and stood next to him, taking turns with him in blowing brandy into the eyes and nostrils of the offside horse. We did this several times.

The predikant asked various questions, to show how interested he was in this old-fashioned method of overcoming fatigue in draught-animals. But what the predikant said at the next stop made me perceive that he was more than a match for a dozen men like Gert Bekker in point of astuteness.

When we stopped the cart, the predikant held up his hand.

"Don't you and your friend trouble to get off this time," the predikant called out when Gert Bekker was once more reaching for the bottle. "The ouderling and I have decided to take turns with you in blowing brandy into the horses' faces. We don't want to put all the hard work on to your shoulders."

We made several more halts after that, with the result that daybreak found us still a long way from Sephton's Nek. In the early dawn we saw the thatched roof of Piet Reilly's house through the thorn-trees some distance from the road. When the predikant suggested that we call at the homestead for coffee, we explained to him that the Reillys were Catholics.

"But isn't Piet Reilly's wife a relative of yours?" the predikant asked of Gert Bekker. "Isn't she your second cousin, or something?"

"They are Catholics," Gert answered.

"Coffee," the predikant insisted.

"Catholics," Gert Bekker repeated stolidly.

The upshot of it was, naturally enough, that we outspanned shortly afterwards in front of the Reilly homestead. That was the kind of man that the predikant was in an argument.

"The coffee will be ready soon," the predikant said as we walked up to the front door. "There is smoke coming out of the chimney."

Almost before we had stopped knocking, Gertruida Reilly had opened both the top and bottom doors. She started slightly when she saw, standing in front of her, a minister of the Dutch Reformed Church. In spite of her look of agitation, Gertruida was still pretty, I thought, after ten years of being married to Piet Reilly.

When she stepped forward to kiss her cousin, Gert Bekker, I saw him turn away, sadly; and I realised something of the shame that she had brought on her whole family through her marriage to a Catholic.

"You looked startled when you saw me, Gertruida," the predikant said, calling her by her first name, as though she was still a member of his congregation.

"Yes," Gertruida answered. "Yes – I was – surprised."

"I suppose it was a Catholic priest that you wanted to come to your front door," Gert Bekker said, sarcastically. Yet there was a tone in his voice that was not altogether unfriendly.

"Indeed, I was expecting a Catholic priest," Gertruida said, leading us into the voorkamer. "But if the Lord has sent the dominee and his ouderling, instead, I am sure it will be well, also."

It was only then, after she had explained to us what had happened, that we understood why Gertruida was looking so troubled. Her eight-year-old daughter had been bitten by a snake: they couldn't tell from the fang-marks if it was a rinkhals or a bakkop. Piet Reilly had driven off in the mule-cart to Vleisfontein, the Catholic mission station, for a priest.

They had cut open and cauterised the wound and had applied red permanganate. The rest was a matter for God. And that was why, when she saw the predikant and the ouderling at her front door, Gertruida believed that the Lord had sent them.

I was glad that Gert Bekker did not at that moment think of mentioning that we had really come for coffee.

"Certainly, I shall pray for your little girl's recovery," the predikant said to Gertruida. "Take me to her."

Gertruida hesitated.

"Will you – will you pray for her the Catholic way, dominee?" Gertruida asked.

Now it was the predikant's turn to draw back.

"But, Gertruida," he said, "you, you whom I myself confirmed in the Enkel-Gereformeerde Kerk in Zeerust – how can you now ask me such a thing? Did you not learn in the catechism that the Romish ritual is a mockery of the Holy Ghost?"

"I married Piet Reilly," Gertruida answered simply, "and his faith is my faith. Piet has been very good to me, Father. And I love him."

We noticed that Gertruida called the predikant 'Father,' now, and not 'Dominee.' During the silence that followed, I glanced at the candle burning before an image of the Mother Mary in a corner of the voorkamer. I looked away quickly from that unrighteousness.

The predikant's next words took us by complete surprise.

"Have you got some kind of prayer-book," the predikant asked, "that sets out the – the Catholic form for a. . . "

"I'll fetch it from the other room," Gertruida answered.

When she had left, the predikant tried to put our minds at ease.

"I am only doing this to help a mother in distress," he explained to the ouderling. "It is something that the Lord will understand. Gertruida was brought up a Dopper girl. In some ways she is still one of us. She does not understand that I have no authority to conduct this Catholic service for the sick."

The ouderling was going to say something.

But at that moment Gertruida returned with a little black book that you could almost have taken for a Dutch Reformed Church psalm-book. Only, I knew that what was printed inside it was as iniquitous as the candle burning in the corner.

Yet I also began to wonder if, in not knowing the difference, a Bapedi really was so very ignorant, even though he walked with his buttocks sticking out.

"My daughter is in this other room," Gertruida said, and started in the direction of the door. The predikant followed her. Just before entering the bedroom he turned round and faced the ouderling.

"Will you enter with me, Brother Erasmus?" the predikant asked.

The ouderling did not answer. The veins stood out on his forehead. On his face you could read the conflict that went on inside him. For what seemed a very long time he stood quite motionless. Then he stooped down to the rusbank for his hat – which he did not need – and walked after the predikant into the bedroom.

Cometh Comet

HANS ENGELBRECHT was the first farmer in the Schweizer-Reneke District to trek (Oom Schalk Lourens said). With his wife and daughter and what was left of his cattle, he moved away to the northern slopes of the Dwarsberge, where the drought was less severe. Afterwards he was joined by other farmers from the same area. I can still remember how untidy the veld looked in those days, with rotting carcasses and sun-bleached bones lying about everywhere. Day after day we had stood at the boreholes, pumping an ever-decreasing trickle of brackish water into the cattle troughs. We watched in vain for a sign of a cloud. And it seemed that if anything did fall out of that sky, it wouldn't do us much good: it would be a shower of brimstone, most likely.

Still, it was a fine time for the aasvoëls and the crows. That was at the beginning, of course. Afterwards, when all the carcasses had been picked bare, and the Boers had trekked, most of the birds of prey flew away, also.

We trekked away in different directions. Four or five families eventually came to a halt at the foot of the Dwarsberge, near the place where Hans Engelbrecht was outspanned. In the vast area of the Schweizer-Reneke District only one man had chosen to stay behind. He was Ocker Gieljan, a young bywoner who had worked for Hans Engelbrecht since his boyhood. Ocker Gieljan spoke rarely, and then his words did not always seem to us to make sense.

Hans Engelbrecht was only partly surprised when, on the morning that the ox-wagon was loaded and the long line of oxen that were skin and bone started stumbling along the road to the north, Ocker Gieljan made it clear that he was not leaving the farm. The native voorloper had already gone to the head of the span and Hans Engelbrecht's wife and his eighteen-year-old daughter, Maria, were seated on the wagon, under the tent-sail, when Ocker Gieljan suddenly declared that he had decided to stay behind on the farm "to look after things here."

This was another instance of Ocker Gieljan's saying something that did not make sense. There could be nothing for him to look after, there, since in the whole district hardly a lizard was left alive.

Hans Engelbrecht was in no mood to waste time in arguing with a daft bywoner. Accordingly, he got the kaffirs to unload half a sack of mealie-meal and a quantity of biltong in front of Ocker Gieljan's mud-walled room.

During the past few years it had not rained much in the Marico Bushveld, either. But there was at least water in the Molopo, and the grazing was fair. Several months passed. Every day, from our camp by the Molopo, we studied the skies, which were of an intense blue. There was no longer that yellow tinge in the air that we had got used to in the Schweizer-Reneke District. But there was never a rain-cloud.

The time came, also, when Hans Engelbrecht was brought to understand that the Lord had visited still more trouble on himself and his family. A little while before we had trekked away from our farms, a young insurance agent had left the district suddenly for Cape Town. That was a long distance to run away, especially when you think of how bad the roads were in those days. And in some strange fashion it seemed to me as though that young insurance agent was actually our leader. For he stood, after all, with his light hat and short jacket, at the head of our flight out of the Schweizer-Reneke area.

It became a commonplace, after a while, for Maria Engelbrecht to be seen seated in the grass beside her father's wagon, weeping. Few pitied her. She must have sat in the grass too often, with that insurance agent with the pointed, polished shoes, Lettie Grobler said to some of the women – forgetting that there had been no grass left in the Schweizer-Reneke veld at the time when Hans Engelbrecht's daughter was being courted.

It was easy for Maria to wipe the tears from her face, another woman said. Easier than to wipe away her shame, the woman meant.

Now and again, from some traveller who had passed through Schweizer-Reneke, we who had trekked out of that stricken region would hear a few useless things about it. We learnt nothing that we did not already know. Ocker Gieljan was still on the Engelbrecht farm, we heard. And the only other living creature in the whole district was a solitary crow. A passing traveller had seen Ocker Gieljan at the borehole. He was pumping water into a trough for the crow, the traveller said.

"When his mealie-meal gives out, Ocker will find his way here, right enough," Hans Engelbrecht growled impatiently.

Then the night came when, from our encampment beside the Molopo, we first saw the comet, in the place above the Dwarsberg rante where the sun had gone down. We all began to wonder what that new star with the long tail meant. Would it bring rain? We didn't know. We could see, of course, that the star was an omen. Even an uneducated kaffir would know that. But we did not know what sort of omen it was.

If the bark of the maroelas turned black before the polgras was in seed, we would know that it would be a long winter. And if a wind sprang up suddenly in the evening, blowing away from the sunset, we would next morning send the cattle out later to graze. We knew many things about the veld and the sky and the seasons. But even the oldest Free State farmer among us didn't know what effect a comet had on a mealie-crop.

Hans Engelbrecht said that we should send for Rev. Losper, the missionary who ministered to the Bechuanas at Ramoutsa. But the rest of us ignored his suggestion.

During the following nights the comet became more clearly visible. A young policeman on patrol in these parts called on us one evening. When we spoke to him about the star, he said that he could do nothing about it, himself. It was a matter for the higher authorities, he said, laughing.

Nevertheless, he had made a few calculations, the policeman explained, and he had sent a report to Pretoria. He estimated that the star was twenty-seven and a half miles in length, and that it was travelling faster than a railway train. He would not be surprised if the star reached Pretoria before his report got there. That would spoil his chances of promotion, he added.

We did not take much notice of the policeman's remarks, however. For one thing, he was young. And, for another, we did not have much respect for the police.

"If a policeman doesn't even know how to get on to the spoor of a couple of kaffir oxen that I smuggle across the Bechuanaland border," Thys Bekker said, "how does he expect to be able to follow the footprints of a star across the sky? That is big man's work."

The appearance of the comet caused consternation among the Bechuanas in the village of Ramoutsa, where the mission station was. It did not take long for some of their stories about the star to reach our encampment on the other side of the Molopo. And although, at first, most of us professed to laugh at what we said were just ignorant kaffir superstitions, yet in the end we also began to share something of the Bechuana's fears.

"Have you heard what the kaffirs say about the new star?" Arnoldus Grobler, husband of Lettie Grobler, asked of Thys Bekker. "They say that it is a red beast with a fat belly like a very great chief, and it is going to come to eat up every blade of grass and every living thing."

"In that case, I hope he lands in Schweizer-Reneke," Thys Bekker said. "If that red beast comes down on my farm, all that will happen is that in a short while there will be a whole lot more bones lying around to get white in the sun."

Some of us felt that it was wrong of Thys Bekker to treat the matter so lightly. Moreover, this story only emanated from Ramoutsa, where there were a mission station and a post office. But a number of other stories, that were in every way much better, started soon afterwards to come out of the wilder parts of the Bushveld, travelling on foot. It seemed that the further a tribe of kaffirs lived away from civilisation, the more detailed and dependable was the information they had about the comet.

I know that I began to feel that Hans Engelbrecht had made the right suggestion in the first place, when he had said that we should send for the missionary. And I sensed that a number of others in our camp shared my feelings. But not one of us wanted to make this admission openly.

In the end it was Hans Engelbrecht himself who sent to Ramoutsa for Rev. Losper. By that time the comet was – each night in its rising – higher in the heavens, and it soon got round that the new star portended the end of the world. Lettie Grobler went so far as to declare that she had seen the good Lord Himself riding in the tail of the comet. What convinced us that she had, indeed, seen the Lord, was when she said that He had on a hat of the same shape as the predikant in Zwartruggens wore.

Lettie Grobler also said that the Lord was coming down to punish all of us for the sins of Maria Engelbrecht. This thought disturbed us greatly. We began to resent Maria's presence in our midst.

It was then that Hans Engelbrecht had sent for the missionary.

Meanwhile, Rev. Losper had his hands full with the Bechuanas at Ramoutsa, who seemed on the point of panicking in earnest. The latest story about the comet had just reached them, and because it had come from somewhere out of the deepest part of Africa, where the natives wore arrows tipped with leopard fangs stuck through their nostrils, like moustaches, it was easily the most terrifying story of all. The story had come to the village, thumped out on the tom-toms.

The Bechuana chief at Ramoutsa – so Rev. Losper told us afterwards – fell into such a terror at the message brought by the speaking drums, that he thrust a handful of earth into his mouth, without thinking. He would have swallowed it, too, the missionary said, if one of his indunas hadn't restrained him in time, pointing out to the chief that perhaps the drum-men had got the message wrong. For, since the post office had come to Ramoutsa, the kaffirs whose work in the village it was to receive and send out messages on their tom-toms had got somewhat out of practice.

Consequently, because of the tumult at Ramoutsa, it happened that Ocker Gieljan arrived at the encampment before Rev. Losper got there.

Ocker Gieljan looked very tired and dusty on that afternoon when he walked up to Hans Engelbrecht's wagon. He took off his hat and, smiling somewhat vacantly, sat down without speaking in the shade of the veld-tent, inside which Maria Engelbrecht lay on a mattress. Neither Hans Engelbrecht nor his wife asked Ocker Gieljan any questions about his journey from the Schweizer-Reneke farm. They knew that he could have nothing to tell.

Shortly afterwards, Ocker Gieljan made a communication to Hans Engelbrecht, speaking diffidently. Thereupon Hans Engelbrecht went into the tent and spoke to his wife and daughter. A few minutes later he came out, looking pleased with himself.

"Sit down here on this riempiestoel, Ocker," Hans Engelbrecht said to his prospective son-in-law, "and tell me how you came to leave the farm."

"I got lonely," Ocker Gieljan answered, thoughtfully. "You see, the crow flew away. I was alone, after that. The crow was then already weak. He didn't fly straight, like crows do. His wings wobbled."

When he told me about this, years later, Hans Engelbrecht said that something in Ocker Gieljan's tone brought him a sudden vision of the way his daughter, Maria, had also left the Schweizer-Reneke District. With broken wings.

I thought that Rev. Losper looked relieved to find, on his arrival at the camp, some time later, that all that was required of him, now, was the performance of a marriage ceremony.

On the next night but one, Maria Engelbrecht's child was born. All the adults in our little trekker community came in the night and the rain – which had been falling steadily for many hours – with gifts for Maria and her child.

And when I saw the star again, during the temporary break in the rain-clouds, it seemed to me that it was not such a new star, at all: that it was, indeed, a mighty old star.

Graven Image

YES, I know those wood-carvings that the kaffirs used to make long ago (Oom Schalk Lourens said). They were very silly things, of course, and I had a good laugh at them myself, more than once. Several of my neighbours, including Karel Nienaber, had a good laugh at them, also, at various times. In fact, when you come to think of it, the one particular thing about those figures that the kaffirs used to carve out of soft wood like kremetart or 'ndubu was that you could always get a good laugh out of them.

And it is singular how into these mirthful incidents there got tangled part of the darker being of Louisa Wessels, a girl who did not laugh. And she seems almost as reluctant now to enter the story as she was then about becoming Karel Nienaber's bride. I can picture Louisa Wessels yet, shy but firm in her withdrawing, and as still as blue water.

It was all right, of course, as long as those wood-carvers stuck to chiselling certain kinds of animals that they knew well. The way they could carve a giraffe, for instance: his long neck, cut out of a piece of mesetla wood with a blunt knife, and the whole of him covered in black spots burnt with a red-hot iron, and his pointed head turned to one side, half upwards – why, you could *see* that giraffe. It was almost as though you could see the leaves of the tree, too, that he was pulling down and eating for his breakfast.

Although we knew that the whole thing was cut out of a piece of Bushveld wood by a lazy Bechuana, who would have been better employed in chopping up that wood and bringing a bundle of it into a farmer's kitchen, nevertheless, we could see that, for all his ignorance, the Bechuana kaffir knew how to carve a giraffe so that it looked really life-like. Because we Marico farmers knew a giraffe when we saw one. And when one of those wood-carvers brought along a model of a giraffe, we would smile to think that that kaffir was so uneducated, but we would also know that the thing he had carved was exactly like a giraffe. Sometimes we could even tell, from the way that the giraffe was standing, as to what particular kind of tree he was eating his breakfast from. Just from the way his head was turned, and the position in which his hind legs were placed, and the manner in which he would droop his shoulders to miss the thorns.

And the wood-carvers would also cut out, joined together on a piece of stick, three wild ducks swimming one behind the other. That was one of their favourite pieces of carving. The way that the ducks sat on the water was very true to life, the front duck swimming with his head high up, since he was naturally proud to be the leader. The only thing that was wrong was that those three wild ducks were held together by a piece of stick. That used to give us a very good laugh. I mean, we had often seen three ducks swimming in a row in that particular way. But they had never been tied together on a piece of stick.

It was when an old Bechuana wood-carver named Radipalong, in Ramoutsa, began carving what he said were the images of various white men living in the Marico, that we really started laughing.

I suppose you know that a kaffir wood-carver will never cut a figure of another kaffir. He's not allowed to. Because, if that kaffir finds out about it, there will be a lot of trouble in the kraal. The kaffirs believe that if you have got an enemy that you want to get rid of, then what you have to do is to make an image of him: it doesn't matter if it is a good likeness or not, as long as you yourself know what is meant by it: and then you hammer something, a strip of brass or an iron nail, into that part of your enemy that you want to get stricken. And the kaffirs say that it always works, when you do that. They say that that is the reason, for instance, why many an unpopular chief has been known to die prematurely, going to his death with a sudden pain in his belly, for which there has been no explanation. And then, later on, in the hut of some enemy of the chief, there has been found a little wooden image with an iron nail driven through its stomach. And how they knew that it was the chief was because something that belonged to him, like a piece of his kaross, was attached to the wooden image... And, also, of course, because the chief had died...

For this reason a kaffir is not very happy when a wood-carver comes along to him with a piece of wood fashioned in the likeness of a human being, and informs him, "This is you." Even when the image hasn't got a piece of brass driven into its belly, the ordinary ignorant kaffir, confronted with his own likeness cut out of wood, will bid the wood-carver tarry a little while in front of the hut – while he goes round to the back to look for his axe.

All of this brings me to that wood-carver in Ramoutsa, Radipalong, who, because the kaffirs would not allow him to carve likenesses of themselves, took it into his head to cut what he thought were images of white people.

There is no doubt about it that when Radipalong, who was very old and emaciated-looking, confined himself to cutting the figures of animals from soft wood – the softer, the better, because you had merely to look at him to see that he did not like exerting himself too much – then what he carved was quite all right. He could carve a hippopotamus, or a rhinoceros, or an elephant, or a yellow-bellied hyena – the more low sort of hyena – in such a way that you *knew* that animal exactly, through your having seen it grazing under a tree, or drinking at a waterhole, or just leaning against an ant-hill without doing anything in particular.

But it was when Radipalong started carving what he imagined, in his kaffir ignorance, to be the likenesses of Boer farmers in this part of the Marico, that we commenced laughing differently from the way we laughed at his wild ducks. Our laughter now seemed to have more meaning in it.

For instance, Radipalong carved what he said was the image of the Dutch Reformed Church missionary at Ramoutsa, Rev. Kriel. That was one of the first good laughs we had, Rev. Kriel joining in loudly – although I thought that his laughter came from rather too deep down.

"See how silly that kaffir, Radipalong, makes me look," Rev. Kriel said to us, one day, after he had conducted a service in Jurie Bekker's farmhouse. "I brought along this carving that he made of me. I brought it along just for fun. I gave him one shilling and ninepence for it, also just for fun. Look how foolishly he makes my collar stand up, right under my ears. And my eyes – so close together. Have you ever seen such a dishonest-looking pair of eyes before? And the way he makes my chin slope backwards from my bottom teeth. . . You should have heard how my wife laughed when I showed her this carving. In fact, every time she sees me now, she laughs. I suppose she feels how incredible it is that, in these times, you can still find as benighted a heathen as that old Radipalong is. And the funny part of it is that he seems to take his ridiculous wood-carving seriously. As though he is carving out a career for himself, I said to my wife. Ha, ha."

We all laughed at that. Ha, ha, we said.

After that, Radipalong made an image of Karel Nienaber. Once more we laughed a good deal. That was in the Nienaber voorhuis, where we were drinking coffee. Old Piet Nienaber's son, Karel, was engaged to be married to Louisa Wessels, and Louisa and her parents, who stayed at Abjaterskop, were on a visit that afternoon to the Nienaber family. A few neighbours had dropped in as well, and, as I have said, there was much laughter when young Karel produced Radipalong's latest piece of woodcarving. The wood that the image was made of was so soft that it was more like cork. Almost like a piece of sponge, I thought. It seemed that Radipalong was getting lazier than ever.

"Just see how low he makes my forehead," Karel Nienaber said, and we all laughed again, at the idea that that kaffir, who could carve a leopard exactly like it was, should be so ignorant when it came to making the image of a white man.

"And look at my ears," Karel added, "the way they stick out. They look as though they have been made for a person twice my size."

Again we all guffawed. All of us, that is, except Louisa Wessels. I noticed that she was not laughing at all. Naturally, this circumstance did not at first appear singular to me. It was only right, I felt, that a young girl should not laugh at seeing her lover made to look ridiculous – even though that kaffir wood-carver did not mean to poke fun at Karel, of course. Radipalong just didn't know any better.

Nevertheless, there was something in Louisa's manner that disturbed me. She seemed too quiet. And when Karel Nienaber said, "Just look at my ears," she had not looked at the wooden likeness that he was holding in his hand. Instead, her dark eyes went actually to her lover's face. For a few moments she appeared to be studying Karel's ears, which did, somehow, in that instant, seem to be somewhat too large for the rest of him.

"And what do you think of the way he has done the rest of me?" Karel Nienaber asked again, and by this time he could hardly talk, he was laughing so much at the kaffir's absurd misrepresentation of his figure. "Why, he makes my body look all clumsy, like a sort of pumpkin. To move, I would have to go on wheels."

Once again I noticed that Louisa Wessels looked at Karel Nienaber and not at the carving. And this time, too, she did not laugh. And so I remembered that young man who had been courting Louisa in the past, and to whom her parents had objected, because they wanted their daughter to marry Karel Nienaber. And I wondered what thoughts were going on behind Louisa's expressionless features, when Karel came up to her and laughingly placed the image in her lap.

"You can look after this for us," Karel said. "I gave Radipalong a piece of roll-tobacco for it, just for fun. I asked him why he used such a white piece of wood to carve my image out of, and what do you think he said?

He said, 'Well, but you are a white man, baas Karel.' And I said, well of course, I was white but I wasn't sick. And then I asked him why he had made me out of such soft wood. And – you know what? – he just didn't answer me at all."

Louisa sat with her eyes lowered. And, as I am talking to you, I can sense how unwillingly she comes into this story, even now.

Anyway, the stupidity of that wood-carver caused a good deal of merriment in the Marico Bushveld for a while. When Radipalong brought me a carving of myself, with a jaw like an aardvark and big, flat feet, I laughed so much that I just pulled the thing away from him roughly, without paying him anything – not even for fun. And when Radipalong gave Hendrik Pretorius *his* likeness, Hendrik was so amused that Radipalong had a lump behind his ear from where Hendrik Pretorius hit him with a piece of wood that was harder than the wood out of which he made the carving.

Shortly afterwards, Radipalong went out of the business of carving images of white men.

The white men laughed too much.

It was some time later that the engagement between Louisa Wessels and Karel Nienaber got broken off. Although nobody knew all the details surrounding the circumstances under which those two young people parted, we had a pretty good general sort of idea. And we were not surprised when, shortly afterwards, Karel Nienaber left the Marico Bushveld to go and work for a blacksmith in Zeerust. He said he felt it wasn't healthy living in the Bushveld, among all those dark trees.

But what we never understood clearly was how Karel Nienaber had come to open the tamboetie kist in which Louisa Wessels was collecting her trousseau. We did know, however, that Karel found, lying on top of the bridal silks and ribbons, the wooden image that Radipalong had carved of him. And, driven into the place where the heart was, were several rusty nails.

Great-uncle Joris

For quite a number of Boers in the Transvaal Bushveld the expedition against Majaja's tribe of Bechuanas – we called them the Platkop kaffirs – was unlucky.

There was a young man with us on this expedition who did not finish a story that he started to tell of a bygone war. And for a good while afterwards the relations were considerably strained between the long-established Transvalers living in these parts and the Cape Boers who had trekked in more recently.

I can still remember all the activity that went on north of the Dwarsberge at that time, with veldkornets going from one farmhouse to another to recruit burghers for the expedition, and with provisions and ammunition having to be got together, and with new stories being told every day about how cheeky the Platkop kaffirs were getting.

I must mention that about that time a number of Boers from the Cape had trekked into the Marico Bushveld. In the Drogedal area, indeed, the recently arrived Cape Boers were almost as numerous as the Transvalers who had been settled here for a considerable while. At that time I, too, still regarded myself as a Cape Boer, since I had only a few years before quit the Schweizer-Reneke District for the Western Transvaal. When the veldkornet came to my farm on his recruiting tour, I volunteered my services immediately.

"Of course, we don't want *everybody* to go on commando," the veldkornet said, studying me somewhat dubiously, after I had informed him that I was from the Cape, and that older relatives of mine had taken part in wars against the kaffirs in the Eastern Province. "We need some burghers to stay behind to help guard the farms. We can't leave all that to the women and children."

The veldkornet seemed to have conceived an unreasonable prejudice against people whose forebears had fought against the Xhosas in the Eastern Province. But I assured him that I was very anxious to join, and so in the end he consented. "A volunteer is, after all, worth more to a fighting force than a man who has to be commandeered against his will," the veldkornet said, stroking his beard. "Usually."

A week later, on my arrival at the big camp by the Steenbokspruit, where the expedition against the Platkop kaffirs was being assembled,

I was agreeably surprised to find many old friends and acquaintances from the Cape Colony among the burghers on commando. There were also a large number of others whom I then met for the first time, who were introduced to me as new immigrants from the Cape.

Indeed, among ourselves we spoke a good deal about this proud circumstance – about the fact that we Cape Boers actually outnumbered the Transvalers in this expedition against Majaja – and we were glad to think that in time of need we had not failed to come to the help of our new fatherland. For this reason the coolness that made itself felt as between Transvaler and Cape Boer, after the expedition was over, was all the more regrettable.

We remained camped for a good number of days beside the Steenbokspruit. During that time I became friendly with Frikkie van Blerk and Jan Bezuidenhout, who were also originally from the Cape. We craved excitement. And when we were seated around the campfire, talking of life in the Eastern Province, it was natural enough that we should find ourselves swapping stories of the adventures of our older relatives in the wars against the Xhosas. We were all three young, and so we spoke like veterans, forgetting that our knowledge of frontier fighting was based only on hearsay. Each of us was an authority on the best way of defeating a Xhosa impi without loss of life to anybody except the members of the impi. Frikkie van Blerk took the lead in this kind of talk, and I may say that he was peculiar in his manner of expressing himself, sometimes. Unfeeling, you might say. Anyway, as the night wore on, there were in the whole Transvaal, I am sure, no three young men less worried than we were about the different kinds of calamities that, in this uncertain world, would overtake a Xhosa impi.

"Are you married, Schalk?" Jan Bezuidenhout asked me, suddenly.

"No," I replied, "but Frikkie van Blerk is. Why do you ask?"

Jan Bezuidenhout sighed.

"It is all right for you," he informed me. "But I am also married. And it is for burghers like Frikkie van Blerk and myself that a war can become a most serious thing. Who is looking after your place while you are on commando, Frikkie?"

Frikkie van Blerk said that a friend and neighbour, Gideon Kotze, had made special arrangement with the veldkornet, whereby he was released from service with the commando on condition that he kept an eye on the farms within a twenty-mile radius of his own.

"The thought that Gideon Kotze is looking after things, in that way, makes me feel much happier," Frikkie van Blerk added. "It is nice for me to know that my wife will not be quite alone all the time."

"Gideon Kotze – " Jan Bezuidenhout repeated, and sighed again.

"What do you mean by that sigh?" Frikkie van Blerk demanded, quickly, a nasty tone seeming to creep into his voice.

"Oh, nothing," Jan Bezuidenhout answered, "oh, nothing at all."

As he spoke he kicked at a log on the edge of the fire. The fine sparks rose up very high in the still air and got lost in the leaves of the thorn-tree overhead.

Frikkie van Blerk cleared his throat. "For that matter," he said in a meaningful way to Jan Bezuidenhout, "you are also a married man. Who is looking after *your* farm – and *your* wife – while you are sitting here?"

Jan Bezuidenhout waited for several moments before he answered.

"Who?" he repeated, "who? Why, Gideon Kotze, also."

This time when Jan Bezuidenhout sighed, Frikkie van Blerk joined in, audibly. And I, who had nothing at all to do with any part of this situation, seeing that I was not married, found myself sighing as well. And this time it was Frikkie van Blerk who kicked the log by the side of the fire. The chunk of white wood, which had been hollowed out by the ants, fell into several pieces, sending up a fiery shower so high that, to us, looking up to follow their flight, the yellow sparks became for a few moments almost indistinguishable from the stars.

"It's all rotten," Frikkie van Blerk said, taking another kick at the crumbling log, and missing.

"There's something in the Bible about something else being something like sparks flying upwards," Jan Bezuidenhout announced. His words sounded very solemn. They served as an introduction to the following story that he told us:

"It was during my grandfather's time," Jan Bezuidenhout said. "My great-uncle Joris, who had a farm near the Keiskamma, had been commandeered to take the field in the Fifth Kaffir War. Before setting out for the war, my great-uncle Joris arranged for a friend and neighbour to visit his farm regularly, in case his wife needed help. Well, as you know, there is no real danger in a war against kaffirs – "

"Yes, we know that," Frikkie van Blerk and I agreed simultaneously, to sound knowledgeable.

"I mean, there's no danger as long as you don't go so near that a kaffir can reach you with an assegai," Jan Bezuidenhout continued. "And, of course, no white man is as uneducated as all that. But what happened to my great-uncle Joris was that his horse threw him. The commando was retreating just about then – "

"To reload," Frikkie van Blerk and I both said, eager to show how well-acquainted we were with the strategy used in kaffir wars.

"Yes," Jan Bezuidenhout went on. "To reload. And there was no time for the commando to stop for my great-uncle Joris. The last his comrades saw of him, he was crawling on his hands and knees towards an aardvark hole. They didn't know whether the Xhosas had seen him. Perhaps the commando had to ride back fast because – "

Jan Bezuidenhout did not finish his story. For, just then, a veldkornet came with orders from Kommandant Pienaar. We had to put out the fire. We had not to make so much noise. We were to hold ourselves in readiness, in case the kaffirs launched a night attack. The veldkornet also instructed Jan Bezuidenhout to get his gun and go on guard duty.

"There was never any nonsense like this in the Cape," Frikkie van Blerk grumbled, "when we were fighting the Xhosas. It seems the Transvalers don't know what a kaffir war is."

By this time Frikkie van Blerk had got to believe that he actually had taken part in the campaigns against the Xhosas.

I have mentioned that there were certain differences between the Transvalers and the Cape Boers. For one thing, we from the Cape had a lightness of heart which the Transvalers lacked – possibly (I thought at the time) because the stubborn Transvaal soil made the conditions of life more harsh for them. And the difference between the two sections was particularly noticeable on the following morning, when Kommandant Pienaar, after having delivered a short speech about how it was our duty to bring book-learning and refinement to the Platkop kaffirs, gave the order to advance. We who were from the Cape cheered lustily. The Transvalers were, as always, subdued. They turned pale, too, some of them. We rode on for the best part of an hour. Frikkie van Blerk, Jan Bezuidenhout and I found ourselves together in a small group on one flank of the commando.

"It's funny," Jan Bezuidenhout said, "but I don't see any kaffirs, anywhere, with assegais. It doesn't seem to be like it was against the Xhosas – "

He stopped abruptly. For we heard what sounded surprisingly like a shot. Afterwards we heard what sounded surprisingly like more shots.

"These Platkop Bechuanas are *not* like the Cape Xhosas," I agreed, then, dismounting.

In no time the whole commando had dismounted. We sought cover in dongas and behind rocks from the fire of an enemy who had concealed himself better than we were doing.

"No, the Xhosas were not at all like this," Frikkie van Blerk announced, tearing off a strip of shirt to bandage a place in his leg from which the blood flowed. "Why didn't the Transvalers let us know it would be like this?"

It was an ambush. Things happened very quickly. It became only too clear to me why the Transvalers had not shared in our enthusiasm earlier on, when we had gone over the rise together, at a canter, through the yellow grass, singing. I was still reflecting on this circumstance, some time later, when our commando remounted and galloped away out of that whole part of the district. To reload, we said, years afterwards, to strangers who asked. The last we saw of Jan Bezuidenhout was after he had had his horse shot down from under him. He was crawling on hands and knees in the direction of an aardvark hole.

"Like great-uncle, like nephew," Frikkie van Blerk said, when we were discussing the affair some time later, back in camp beside the Steenbokspruit. Frikkie van Blerk's unfeeling sally was not well received.

Thus ended the expedition against Majaja, that brought little honour to the commando that took part in it. There was not a burgher who retained any sort of a happy memory of the affair. And for a good while afterwards the relations were strained between Transvaler and Cape Boer in the Marico.

It was with a sense of bitterness that, some months later, I had occasion to call to mind the fact that Gideon Kotze, the man appointed to look after the farms of the burghers on commando, was a Transvaler.

And when I saw Gideon Kotze sitting talking to Jan Bezuidenhout's widow, on the front stoep of their house, I wondered what the story was, about his great-uncle Joris, that Jan Bezuidenhout had not been able to finish telling.

The Old Potchefstroom Gaol

You can always get people to listen to a story with a murder and a hanging in it (Oom Schalk Lourens said). And it doesn't matter, then, if it is even quite an ordinary sort of murder. Nor are people particular if the hanging is not so very up-to-date, either. They can stand it.

The authorities ordered the old gaol in Potchefstroom to be rebuilt because it was damp; and neither light nor air could get into it. And it was very unhealthy. Many people considered that this was a foolish step on the part of the authorities, rebuilding the place. After all, what was the good of a prison if it *wasn't* unhealthy?

The prisoners from behind the bars of their cells saw the outer walls of the prison being pulled down. And they started getting hopeful. But the look of expectancy went from their faces when they were shortly afterwards moved to another prison. With the walls down, the gallows in the courtyard stood revealed. And so the story of Karel Malan and Thys Burkhardt – and of Wiesie van Breda – was recalled as clearly as though the gallows had been erected only yesterday, and not half a century before.

You might think, perhaps, that an old gaol is a strange setting for the story of a courtship. But when it is young love, in the springtime – why, the gates of a prison can help a good deal to make it impressive. Young hearts and an old gaol. I've seen it happen here, in the Marico Bushveld. And I have seen the same thing in the bioscope in Zeerust. Maybe the best kind of love story *is* when it's round a prison.

Wiesie van Breda had been betrothed to Karel Malan, the young Sunday school teacher, a good while before she attracted the attention of Thys Burkhardt, who was not like a Sunday school teacher at all. For when Thys Burkhardt laughed in the bar you could hear him as far as Suid Street.

Then one Sunday morning Thys Burkhardt was found lying in the vlei with a Mauser bullet in his heart. And for Karel Malan a class sat waiting, on the hard benches of a Sunday school, a long while, in vain.

Karel Malan was tried for the murder of Thys Burkhardt and was sentenced to be hanged.

That was why Karel Malan would not one day be coming out of the church with Wiesie van Breda's hand tucked under his arm, the members of the congregation throwing rice. It was all just because what Karel Malan carried in the bend of his arm was not his hymn-book – on that Sunday morning when he went through the vlei looking for Thys Burkhardt.

And the story that got spread about Karel Malan, later on, was that he was never hanged. He had family – and church – influence, it was said. And on the night preceding the morning set down for his execution he was smuggled out of the prison in time to get on the mail-coach for the Cape, the hangman walking in front, carrying Karel Malan's portmanteau as far as the coach station for him.

There was not much evidence in support of this story – as there never is, in such matters, I have noticed. But then, it was not likely that a condemned man would be smuggled out of a prison at night in such a way that everybody could see it being done. The authorities would not have moved Karel Malan out of the prison as openly as they were, fifty years later, to move all the convicts to another place of confinement – the authorities even allowing the Salvation Army to distribute tracts to the prisoners as they came out of the front gate. The municipal refuse span used very bad language, that time, about all the religious leaflets they had to sweep up that the more hardened convicts threw away in the street.

About all there was to go by, with regard to Karel Malan having been smuggled out of gaol, was the statement made by the driver of the Cape stage-coach. The driver said that he had a passenger aboard from the Transvaal who sang Sunday school hymns right as far into the Karoo as Matjesfontein, at which place the passenger got hoarse.

When a responsible citizen in the Potchefstroom saloon bar put him the question, the driver of the stage-coach said, yes, he did notice that the passenger had a portmanteau. But he wouldn't know whether a hangman had carried it for some distance. He hadn't taken a proper look at the handle of the portmanteau, the stage-coach driver said.

The other piece of evidence was that Warder Visagie – who had not been at the Potchefstroom gaol above a month or two – was suddenly transferred to Pretoria. And people said it was because he talked too much.

Well, it was true enough that Warder Visagie was talking quite a lot about then. But his talk was mostly about a girl with ringlets, who lived next door to the boarding-house in which he was staying, and with whom he had fallen in love, having seen her a few times on the other side of the galvanised-iron fence; and who didn't seem to want him; and whose name he didn't know, even, he being too shy to ask – contenting himself, instead, with throwing her an orange.

"I honestly don't know anything about a hanging in the gaol just lately," Warder Visagie announced in the saloon bar. "I mean, if there was a hanging I would have known, wouldn't I? Especially if it was a white man, as you say. . . What? Oh, *him*. Well, I mean, I never worried much about Karel Malan. With nothing more on his mind than a hanging, Karel Malan couldn't know what real trouble was. I tell you, her hair is all in ringlets. And I could never work up enough courage to talk to her, even. And then I threw her that ripe orange for a present. And it had to be my luck that it should hit her on her left ear, just as she was walking back into the kitchen. And she said to me, 'Why don't you — ' And she slammed the kitchen door shut behind her."

Warder Visagie sighed deeply, then, in that old saloon bar in which a shining paraffin lamp had a few months earlier taken the place of a row of candles.

"She's got dark eyes," Warder Visagie said after a pause, "as far as I can see from my side of the fence. And she's got ringlets. And her eyes turn up at the corners when she laughs."

"I should think she must laugh a good deal," the bartender said, drily, "looking at what's on the other side of the fence."

Because he didn't catch on, the patrons of the saloon bar understood that Warder Visagie really was in love. His face that was flushed with brandy was also strangely shadowed under the paraffin lamp.

All those stories were remembered, in great detail, fifty years later, at the rebuilding of the old gaol. The Potchefstroom public walked about the prison terrain, after the front walls had been demolished, with a freedom that even a prison governor of long standing would never have dared assume and that even the oldest convict would not have permitted himself, as long as he had any appearance to keep up.

The first thing that struck visitors from the town about the prison was the fine state of preservation of the gallows. Riem Pienaar summed it up in these words: "They don't make gallows like that these days. Today, they would never use that class of wood anymore."

But it was just like Riem Pienaar to talk that way, of course, as though he knew everything: in this case, he was talking as an authority on being hanged. The truth was, however, that with the years Riem Pienaar had gained an ascendancy with the citizens of Potchefstroom, just through making statements that nobody thought of questioning.

"All the same," Riem Pienaar asserted, "if Karel Malan really had been hanged, the gallows wouldn't have looked nearly so new. You've got no idea how old a gallows gets to look, suddenly, just from having had a white man hanged from it."

Nobody tried to argue with Riem Pienaar. From past experience they knew it was useless.

Now, it was just at this time, too, that the Sunday school building had to be extended and repaired. The thatched roof had to be replaced by galvanised iron. And it so happened that the contract for the work on the Sunday school building was given to the same builder who was renovating the gaol. The price he had quoted the church was so low.

There was some dissatisfaction among a section of churchgoers, however, when they discovered why the builder could make the extensions to the Sunday school so cheaply. They found he was using the building materials from the gaol.

When the matter was put to him the builder affected surprise.

"Why, there's no better timber in the country for the rafters than what I'm taking out of the gaol," he said. "It's real stinkwood. And as good as when it was put up. Where can you get timber like that today?"

He said he would also have used the windows of the gaol for the Sunday school. Only, he added, the gaol had no windows. It was not the sort of gaol that went in for fresh air.

Nevertheless, the protests began again when the builder had the gallows cut down, as well, and got the kaffirs to carry the gallows timber across the way to the Sunday school.

"Why, it's real oak," he said. "This wood is as solid as the day they hanged Karel Malan on it. It's also seasoned."

The builder seemed surprised that his arguments did not silence the protests.

It was in the midst of this unpleasantness that it became known that the Sunday school was being haunted by Karel Malan's ghost. You could understand that, with his gallows gone, the murderer of Thys Burkhardt would not be able to rest in peace. Karel Malan had got used to his gallows standing there for over half a century. That was what some people said. Others said again that why Karel Malan was haunting the Sunday school building was because he himself had been a

Sunday school teacher. His spirit was unhappy at the builder's desecration of the place of worship in which he had worked earnestly in the old days.

Those who had seen the ghost of Karel Malan all described it in the same way. It was the ghost of an old man with a long white beard. This was a sufficiently singular circumstance. How could Karel Malan's ghost grow old like that, if he had been hanged in his early manhood?

A few days later the builder's kaffirs found a very old man with a white beard walking about the Sunday school building where they were busy extending a wall. And they were in deadly fear, the kaffirs said. For they thought that the old man with the white beard was from the Works Department, and that he would discover that the mortar they were mixing consisted of six wheelbarrow-loads of river sand to one shovelful of cement.

In a few minutes a small band had gathered about the old man. He was plied with questions. "Are you really Karel Malan?" "Did you murder Thys Burkhardt?" "Is it true that you escaped the night before you were going to be hanged?"

The old man could answer only falteringly. He had forgotten most of the early years of his life, he said. But he knew he had lived in Potchefstroom as a young man. Certain scenes were still familiar to him.

The builder tapped his forehead.

"The old Oom is clearly in his second childhood," the builder said. "But maybe he is after all Karel Malan. And there is one person alone who can prove it – Tant Wiesie van Breda."

It was quite a procession that moved off shortly, with the white-bearded old man and the builder at the front, in the direction of Wiesie van Breda's cottage.

Riem Pienaar thoughtfully went on ahead to prepare Wiesie van Breda's mind beforehand. She mustn't faint, but her dead lover was at that moment coming up the street, some people with him, Riem Pienaar warned Wiesie van Breda.

It took quite a lot of rooi laventel and a cup of water to bring Wiesie van Breda round again, because of Riem Pienaar's tactful words. And when the elderly stranger came in at the front gate, the crowd around him having grown quite considerably, Wiesie van Breda was able to take a good look at him and to assure the bystanders that he wasn't Karel Malan.

Riem Pienaar looked a very disappointed man.

"Could he – " Riem Pienaar asked after a pause, "could he perhaps be the other one? Thys Burkhardt, that is?" His voice did not sound very hopeful.

In the meantime, although the stranger was not Karel Malan come back from the past, Wiesie van Breda nevertheless falteringly held out her hand to him.

The elderly stranger was the first to talk.

"What did you mean when you said to me, 'Why don't you —?'" the old man asked. "You've still got ringlets. . . ."

"I meant, 'Why don't you come round to the front door and knock?'" Wiesie van Breda answered. "Where's that funny blue uniform you used to wear, with the flat cap?"

"Your eyes still turn up like that at the corners when you laugh," the old man said. "I'm on pension and I've come to settle down here," ex-Warder Visagie added, during all that time not letting go of Wiesie van Breda's hand.

Notes on the Text

THE principal sources for the stories were the versions first published in South African periodicals in the 1930s and 1940s (see the listing below). Thirteen of the stories were published only once before being collected into book form. In these cases the editorial procedure was simply to follow the original periodical publication, with minor corrections being made in the case of obvious typographical errors. Inconsistencies in spelling and style were also routinely adjusted. (One 'correction' requires explanation. "The Wind in the Tree" has always appeared in posthumous collections as "The Wind in the Trees" – the assumption perhaps being that the title as it originally appeared in *The S. A. Opinion* was a misprint. If so, the error was made twice: once in the main heading and a second time on top of the column in which the story was continued several pages on in the issue. I have reverted to the original here – as it appears in its *S. A. Opinion* printing – as I think the use of the singular by Bosman was quite deliberate.)

Five of the remaining seven stories ("Veld Fire", "The Ramoutsa Road", "Marico Moon", "Seed-time and Harvest" and "Graven Image") appeared twice in periodicals. In three cases ("Veld Fire", "The Ramoutsa Road" and "Marico Moon") the second published versions were used as copy-texts, the rationale being that Bosman was himself responsible for any revisions that were made and that these later versions were therefore those that he himself preferred. "Marico Moon" first appeared as "Thorn Trees in the Wind", but its new title has been used here as, again, it was presumably the one Bosman preferred.

"Graven Image" appeared twice in virtually identical versions, one in *On Parade* in August, 1948, the other in the same periodical in January, 1952, upon the occasion of Bosman's death. The latter printing was accompanied by the following note: "The story, 'Graven Image,' by the late Herman Charles Bosman is the only one he wrote in English for 'On Parade' and appeared in 1950. At the request of his many admirers, it is reprinted below. – Ed." That editor, Ehrhardt Planjé, otherwise astute and reliable, made two errors here. Bosman published several other stories in English in *On Parade*, including "The Old Transvaal Story" (September,

1948) and "Peaches Ripening in the Sun" (February, 1951). The date of the first appearance of "Graven Image" is also incorrect (actually August, 1948). I have followed this first printing as it had fewer typographical errors.

"Seed-time and Harvest" also appeared twice, but in this case in very different versions. It was first published in *The S. A. Opinion* in December, 1946, and then in *On Parade* in October, 1948 (another story Planjé missed). In following the first of these versions, I have broken with the principle of taking as my copy-text the last published version (and therefore presumably Bosman's preferred one). The reason is quite simply that the *S. A. Opinion* version is better. It is slightly longer, but the additional material is rich and undoubtedly enhances the story. Bosman's characteristic parings in the interests of greater economy and tautness do not, in my opinion, achieve the desired effect in this instance. Lionel Abrahams clearly came to the same conclusion: he used the *S. A. Opinion* version in both his *Unto Dust* (1963) and *Bosman at his Best* (1965) editions.

The remaining two stories ("The Ghost at the Drift" and "The Old Potchefstroom Prison") were both edited from original typescripts held by the Harry Ransom Humanities Research Center in Austin, Texas. "The Ghost at the Drift" appeared in Afrikaans as "Dit Spook by die Drif" in *Die Brandwag* in April, 1948. No published English version has been traced, but a complete typescript with emendations by Bosman is held by the HRHRC and was used as the source here. There was one minor change made: the preposition "by" in the title was altered to the more correct "at."

The case of "The Old Potchefstroom Gaol" is far more complicated. The story was never completed by Bosman, and no evidence of publication of this story (or any variation thereof) has been discovered. The HRHRC holds two manuscripts and a typescript relating to the story. The first of these is seven pages in Bosman's hand, with numerous emendations, in which one version of the story is told. This version is complete, but its conclusion is markedly different from, and less engaging than, the version that appears here. It is also clearly only a first draft: it contains numerous errors and emendations and Bosman had obviously not yet decided how the story should end. The second manuscript is a reworking of this, but only two complete pages of this version survive (probably the first and the third pages), with two further pages containing some notes and an alternative ending. The typescript is based on this second draft, and is far more coherent and resolved than the first manuscript. It does contain numerous holograph emendations, however, and ends abruptly about two-thirds of the way through the story.

The typescript provided the basis for the first part of the story as it is rendered here. The second half of the first manuscript was then used as a 'bridge' between the unfinished typescript and the revised ending in the (incomplete) second manuscript. Inconsistencies among the three drafts were ironed out (characters' names, and the timing of events, for instance) and a coherent story thus fashioned. Although considerable editorial intervention was thus required in order to create a complete version of this story, all of the words in it (with the exception of the title, which I provided) are Bosman's own.

Versions of stories used as copy-texts here. Reprints followed, where applicable, except in the case of "Seed-time and Harvest" and "Graven Image" (see explanation above):

1. "Veld Fire." *New LSD* 1.2 (3 Apr 1931): 2; reprinted *Sjambok* 3.2 (11 Aug 1939): 12-13.

2. "Francina Malherbe." *New LSD* 1.6 (1 May 1931): 5.

3. "The Ramoutsa Road." *New LSD* 1.8 (16 May 1931): 11-12; reprinted *Sjambok* 3.7 (15 Sept 1939): 12-14.

4. "Karel Flysman." *African Magazine* 1.1 (June 1931): 379-381.

5. "Visitors to Platrand." *SAO* 2.1 (1 Nov 1935): 10-12.

6. "Marico Moon." *SAO* 3.3 (28 Nov 1936): 13-14, as "Thorn Trees in the Wind"; reprinted *Trek* 13.4 (Apr 1949): 14-15.

7. "Bushveld Romance." *SAO* 3.13 (17 Apr 1937): 9-10.

8. "On to Freedom." *SAO* 3.20 (24 July 1937): 8-9.

9. "Martha and the Snake." *Ringhals* 3.3 (13 Oct 1939): 8-9.

10. "Concertinas and Confetti." *SAO* (New series) 1.2 (Apr 1944): 20-21, 32.

11. "The Story of Hester van Wyk." *SAO* 1.4 (June 1944): 9-11.

12. "The Wind in the Tree." *SAO* 1.11 (Jan 1945): 18-19, 28.

13. "Camp-fires at Nagmaal." *SAO* 2.4 (June 1945): 14-15, 31.

14. "Seed-time and Harvest." *SAO* 3.10 (Dec 1946): 18-19, 27; reprinted *On Parade* (1 Oct 1948): 8.

* 15. "The Ghost at the Drift." Undated typescript, Harry Ransom Humanities Research Center. Published in Afrikaans as "Dit Spook by die Drif", *Die Brandwag* 11.550 (16 Apr 1948): 9, 38, 40-41.

16. "Dopper and Papist." *Trek* 12.3 (Mar 1948): 22-23, 31.

17. "Cometh Comet." *Trek* 12.6 (June 1948): 16-17.

18. "Graven Image." *On Parade* (6 Aug 1948): 8; reprinted *On Parade* (31 Jan 1952): 7, 17.

19. "Great-uncle Joris." *Trek* 12.10 (Dec 1948): 14-15, 29.

20. "The Old Potchefstroom Gaol." Undated typescript, HRHRC; title supplied.

---

* This story has been placed slightly out of publication sequence because it forms an ideal preface for "Dopper and Papist", with which it can be paired.